THE Average GIRL

ANGELINA GOODE

THE AVERAGE GIRL

Beach Blanket Publishing

www.beachblanketpublishing.com

Printed in the United States of America

Publisher's Note: This is a work of fiction. Names, characters, businesses, places, events and incidents are either the products of the author's imagination or used in a fictitious manner. Any resemblance to actual persons, living or dead, or actual events is purely coincidental.

Book design by Scarlett Rugers Design www.scarlettrugers.com

The Average Girl/ Angelina Goode

First Edition

ISBN 978-0-9961769-0-3 (e-book)

ISBN 978-0-9961769-1-0 (paperback)

To My Girls
You will always be above average to me

Contents

Acknowledgements

I am so thankful for my family and friends and their willing ears that let me go on and on about this book. Their support has been tremendous. My thanks to my husband who keeps me striving for more; my parents for always encouraging me to write; Christine who read and re-read every version of this book that I could possibly think of and replied to innumerable emails regarding the most minute details; Erin who gave me her honest input and helped me brainstorm; and to the friends that I ran endless titles, character names, and scenarios by. Thank you to Scarlett Rugers for a fantastic book cover and to M.B. for showing me that changing a simple word (or two) can make an entire paragraph shine. Thank you to all the teachers that encouraged me to dig deeper and sift out all the unnecessary "stuff."

Finally, I would like to thank NKOTB. Without their music, concerts, and fans to inspire me, this book probably would not exist. Thank you for growing up to be exactly what all your fans expected you to be.

And of course, the biggest thank you of all to my two girls. H, who's imagination and smile inspire me daily, and T, who took extra long naps in my arms as I typed with one hand.

CHAPTER
1

I SIT QUIETLY AT THE STARBUCKS on the corner of Wilshire and Santa Monica Boulevard, pretending to work on my laptop. Two tables away from me and next to the condiment counter sits my client, Sarah, drinking coffee and pretending to read a book. This is our second day at this Starbucks and we have already been here for forty minutes. I am beginning to wonder if we should re-evaluate our plan.

Suddenly a wave of hushed excitement spreads through the store. Everyone's eyes are glued to the swinging front doors as Ryan Scott strides through with his shoulders back and chin up. Everyone's eyes, that is, but Sarah's. She looks at me without turning her head, and I give her the tiniest of nods before spinning back around to stare. She responds to my nod by feigning interest in her Jane Austen novel.

Great Sarah! Keep calm. I know you want to burst inside, but play it cool.

Ryan's eyes quickly scan the room. Before they return to the menu board, they briefly linger on Sarah, the only person who appears *not* to notice him. He orders his grande latte with a double shot of espresso and leans smugly against the counter with his arms folded across his chest. He appears to be staring into space, yet every few moments his eyes fall back to Sarah, who has still *not* looked up from her book.

The barista calls his name, and he pauses to make sure everyone hears it before he reaches for the drink. When he turns around, Sarah is beginning to pack her things, leaving the Austen novel on the table. He heads toward the condiment counter for his regular three sugars. Just as we had rehearsed, Sarah stands up, still focused on packing up, and he tries to pass her. He stops for a moment, Sarah blocking his way.

Thank goodness these celebrities are creatures of habit. It makes my job so much easier.

"Oh, I'm sorry, I didn't see you there." She breathes calmly as she speaks to him. She slings her navy-blue Coach bag over her shoulder and smiles, her head leaning to the side, her eyes soft.

"That's all right," Ryan responds. He stands waiting for her to move but blocks her exit. He half smiles at her.

"Okay then." Sarah glances toward the door behind him, still smiling.

"Oh, now I'm in your way," he declares as he steps aside and watches Sarah move toward the door. "Wait, hey, your book!"

I exhale. The one contingency worked as planned. Should be easy from here on out, as long as she sticks to the script.

She stops and turns back, hiding her smile. Ryan stands there, holding her book in his hands. "Jane Austen, huh." He smirks. "I'm shooting a movie based on one of her books next month."

"Oh, you're an actor. What book?" she asks, pretending not to know.

"*Pride and Prejudice.*" He seems intrigued by Sarah's indifference. "Well, here you go—" He ends his sentence by fishing for her name.

"Sarah," she finishes for him.

"Sarah," he repeats, revealing a slow, sexy smile, "maybe we can have a cup of coffee next time." He holds out the book but is not loosening his grip.

"Yes, maybe." She takes the book from him, and he lets her. "Thanks." Then she is out the door. Ryan turns and grabs his three sugars, looking around the room again to make sure everyone is still watching. Before he finishes stirring them in, I am out on the street and dialing Sarah's cell number.

"Wow! That was unbelievable! I can't believe it worked!" she cries.

"You were awesome! Did you see the way he looked at you?" I ask.

"Yes! I did!" She pauses. "Thank you so much, Olivia. You really made my dream come true. I mean, I never could have done this without you. I'm going to recommend you to all my friends," she rattles on.

Thrilled that all went as planned, I head back down Santa Monica Boulevard toward my office.

A tall, gawky girl in her late teens stands in the waiting room. She has a goofy smile and frizzy brown hair. She shyly stares back at me through her outdated glasses, waiting for an invitation into my office as she taps her arm softly, rattling her bracelet.

"You must be Becky." I gesture for her to enter.

She is young, just out of high school and reminds me a lot of myself when I was a teenager and hanging around outside Brad Griffin's hotel, waiting for my moment.

"So I hear you can work miracles." She sits down softly in the big purple armchair and looks at me, her face filled with hope.

Her innocence brings to mind just how far I've come. Five years ago when I started this business, meeting clients at coffee shops and working out of my apartment, I had no idea what a demand there would be for my services. I always knew people wanted to meet celebrities, but I quickly learned they were willing to *pay* quite a bit for that privilege, especially if they could meet them in a way that didn't make them look foolish. And when it comes to fans, the saying "birds of a feather flock together" has never been more true. Almost all my clients, like Becky, find me through past clients.

I sit behind my desk, folding my hands and smiling. "That's what they say. I help my clients realize a plan that will manifest their greatest dreams. I help everyday people, like you, meet big-time celebrities in a situation that's comfortable for everyone. You get to be yourself, and the celebrity doesn't even know you're a fan."

Becky nods, encouraging me to continue.

"I do all of the research and planning, everything from facilitating a makeover to word-feeding into earpieces, if necessary. The perfect scenario? I arrange for you to 'accidentally' meet your idol in an unremarkable but cute way. If the meeting goes extremely well, I can help arrange another 'accidental' meeting. Many of my clients, though, are happy with a simple encounter. Just knowing that, for a few moments, their idol's attention was focused exclusively on them in some normal, average way is enough."

"Well," Becky says, "I'll need a miracle because even if I do run into Robert Collins, I don't think he'd so much as glance in my direction." Her expression momentarily shows defeat, and then she looks down briefly and smiles again. "I grew up with my dad, and his sense of style is, well," she points to her dark purple and black-striped turtleneck and brown plaid pants, "I guess you could say style was low on the priority list."

"I wouldn't worry too much about style; that's fixable," I assure her. *I must look intimidating to her in my high heels, fitted blouse, and tailored pants.*

"So you can help me?"

"As long as you're eighteen or over, I can help you."

She nods encouragingly.

I slide my welcome packet across the desk. "First we have to get through some paperwork. You know, stuff my lawyer makes you sign." We go through the document page by page. First she must acknowledge that I will help her meet her idol and nothing more, and that there are no guarantees. Then we go through the confidentiality clause: She is not ever to mention my services to anyone (unless it's a referral), especially not to her idol. I am always cautious when I first meet a client. Since a large part of my success depends on anonymity, I can't risk working with anyone who might publicize what I do to celebrities.

Next is the "no stalking" policy. I don't provide home addresses or phone numbers, and if my clients demonstrate any stalker qualities, I immediately cancel our agreement with no refunds. Finally, if the idol is mean or rude, I am not responsible. This section of the contract is particularly important when meeting the celebrity who Becky is interested in.

"How much is this going to cost me?" she asks.

"Well, it all depends what path we take. We can do the—"

"I don't just want to bump into him: I want Robert to notice and remember me; I want to be beautiful. Whatever it costs. I've finally received my mom's inheritance, and she died fifteen years ago. What do you recommend we start with?"

I hesitate. I don't want to insult Becky, but there is a lot of work to do. Robert Collins is notorious for being, well, a prick, to put it nicely. The last client who I helped "accidentally" meet him was abruptly knocked over by his dog. And he didn't so much as offer to help her up. He just looked at her nursing her twisted ankle and walked on by. Luckily that particular client was satisfied with the honor of being able to tell everyone about "the time she got run over by Robert Collins' dog." The only upside of Becky choosing to meet Robert Collins is that he's the star of *Little Town, Big People*, his own sit-com, which means he is often out and about and seems to stick to a regular schedule.

"Well, I should warn you, Robert is pretty well known for—"

"He's a jerk. I know. I'm a huge fan. I've read it all. He punches photographers, flips off journalists, and refuses autographs. That's why I need to be spectacular, not…this. I get that. I just need you to help facilitate it."

I can't help but wonder what a sweet girl like Becky sees in a celebrity with such a bad—and accurate—reputation. Part of me wants to take her under my wing and help build her confidence. Help her find a *real* guy, a real *nice* guy. Or help her realize she doesn't need a guy at all. But that's not my job. So I push all the helpful thoughts out of my head and focus on the task at hand.

"Right." I look Becky over again. She may not be winning any awards for style, but she is smart. "Okay, then the best way to do this is for you to forget you like him."

"What?"

"For you to be spectacular, as you put it, in his eyes, you can't be a fan. You need to be just some average girl." I get up and walk around my desk. I sit in the lavender armchair next to her. "Unless you want to have sex with him just once and never hear from him again. In which case, please, fall all over him. But that's not the kind of service that I provide."

She leans forward in the chair, intrigued.

I continue. "You need to be the kind of girl who doesn't appear to care that he's in front of her. Act like he's in your way. *That* will get his attention."

"You want me to be rude?" She looks at me with a wrinkled brow.

"No, not rude. Just nonchalant," I correct her.

Becky wrinkles her lips and nose, deep in thought. "Hmmm. I never looked at it that way."

"And that's why you've come to me." I give her a reassuring smile as I rest my hand on her arm.

"Okay," she starts, "this could work." Hope is growing in her eyes.

"Let's get started then." I reach out my hand, and she shakes it.

I finish making all of Becky's appointments and set another date to meet with her. "Your homework is to get every bit of information you can on Robert Collins. Legally, of course. I have a lot, but who knows, you may come up with something I haven't come across."

"Great!" Becky yelps as she grabs her pleather bag and stands up. "I can't wait!"

My file on Robert Collins is pretty thick with information and previous clients' results. In my five years facilitating accidental meetings, not one that involved Robert Collins ended how I had hoped. At least Becky is going into this with realistic expectations. I start looking through my notes.

"Walks his German shepherd every morning," *not trying that ploy again.* "Gets Mercedes-Benz washed every Tuesday," *unless Becky has a very expensive car, probably not a good idea to meet there.* "Visits (allegedly) psychologist every Wednesday," *not useful…unless, nah, forget it.* "Gets manicure every Thursday morning," *this is a possibility.*

After drawing out a loose plan for Becky, I flip through a tabloid, looking for more information on Collins; where I stop short on page twenty-three. Right there, midway down, is a picture of the happy couple—the woman starting to show her "baby bump," as the writer puts it. This isn't just any couple, though; this is Brad Griffin and his noncelebrity wife, essentially the couple that, unknowingly, started me in this business. His bright blue eyes jump off the page as much as they did on his posters, which adorned the walls of my teenage bedroom. He has definitely aged but is still as sexy as he was when I, along with millions of other teenage girls, screamed our hearts out as he belted out his pop ballads on the stage.

I can clearly remember claiming my spot with the throngs of fans outside his hotel, hoping he would make an appearance, at which time he would, of course, take one look at me, see what a big fan I was and fall instantly in love, and we would live happily ever after.

Clearly none of that happened, and I know now, it rarely if ever does. Instead, he waited until his popularity died down and found a cute young lawyer who probably never even thought of driving by his hotel. They got married two years later, and that's when it dawned on me: Celebrities don't want to marry, or even date, a "fan." They don't care how many concerts you've been to or how many times you've seen their movies. They want a normal, average girl and a normal, average relationship—they want a normal, average life.

The day of Brad Griffin's wedding, I decided to do for other women what I wish someone had done for me.

I can still feel the blood rushing to my cheeks when I think about how naïve I was, waiting outside a hotel in a tour T-shirt. Not to say he didn't appreciate my (and everyone else's) fandom. It was just not going to get me where I so badly wanted to be—by Brad's side.

Sillier still, as I linger over Brad Griffin's photograph, I feel my heart starting to race.

In order for my business to work, I have to be calm and collected around celebrities. Otherwise I could never be successful at my job.

But Brad Griffin is one celebrity who, even to this day, I couldn't keep it together if I saw him.

This, however, I've decided to think of as an asset since it feeds my passion for my work. Remembering how strongly I once felt about a celebrity helps me relate to my clients and sell my service. Balancing empathy with the fact that I would *never* fall for a celebrity keeps me levelheaded so I can get the job done.

The phone starts ringing and brings me back to reality. I take a gulp of soda and turn the page.

"Olivia Fowler speaking," I chirp into the phone.

It's Maria, my best friend. We have plans tonight to go to James Beach, a popular but mellow bar by the beach. My brother, Preston, and his friend Charlie are joining us, as usual. "We still on for tonight?" she asks.

"Yeah, I'm gonna head home in a bit. Want to grab dinner before?" Maria only lives two blocks from me, so impromptu dinners are common.

"Wish I could. I need to stay a little longer and help my boss with some stuff. Something wrong? You don't sound quite as chipper as usual." There is no point in hiding anything from Maria. "Oh, I know. You read the tabloid, didn't you?"

"Yep. The happy couple is pregnant." I sigh.

"Just remember, Liv. If it wasn't for that very lucky baby mama, you would still be fetching coffee and punching numbers into a calculator for a boring, old accounting executive, instead of running your own business." An accountant herself, she is practical by nature and often provides a reality check. Maria comes from the *everything happens for a reason* school of thinking.

"I know, but give me some credit. I'd like to think that after five years, I wouldn't *still* be fetching coffee." I giggle into the phone.

"We hope," she giggles back. "I'll see you at nine."

CHAPTER
2

I CAN HEAR THE MUSIC PLAYING across the street as I get out of my car. I feed dollar bills into the parking lot pay machine and glance around, searching for a familiar car, though don't find it.

Apparently I'm the first one here. James Beach is in an inconspicuous building on a dark street in the residential area of Venice. If not for the music pouring out of the open door, you'd never know there's a bar there. Every month, Preston, Charlie, Maria, and I get together at one of our favorite hangouts. This one happens to be Charlie's. Even though he lives on the other side of town, he still comes here whenever possible. Maria and I occasionally join him.

When I get to the door, I smile at the bouncer, and he winks back, moving aside to let me in. It's not too crowded for a Friday night. I make my way to an empty stool at the bar. I'm about to order a drink when I'm interrupted.

"She'll have a Tom Collins, and I'll take a Jack and Coke," he says to the bartender, and then faces me. "That's still your drink, right?"

I turn to see a tall curly-headed blond smiling at me. "Charlie! I thought I was the first one here! I didn't see your car outside." I've known Charlie, or maybe I should say Charlie has known me, my entire life. He and my brother met in preschool and have been best friends ever since. He likes to tease me by reminding me that I used to run around the house singing Barry Manilow songs, wearing my mom's nighties. There are videos to prove it. Thanks, mom.

"I got a new car when I got promoted. Has it really been that long since we've hung out?" He leans over and gives me a big hug. "Let's go find a table." I open my purse to pay for my drink, but he motions for me not to. He grabs both our drinks and leads us to an empty table on a ledge above the main floor.

"You got promoted? That's great! Preston didn't tell me!" I hold up my glass toward his and yell "cheers!"

After he takes a swig, he leans over. "I'm an actual publicist. No more administrative work. It's pretty cool. Instead of running copies and putting together gift bags for the big boss, I have people putting gift bags together and running copies for me. I'll even get to plan some big events in a few months."

"That's amazing." I smile at Charlie, and he smiles back.

He opens his mouth to say something.

"Hey, friends!" I look up to see Maria waving her arms at us; Preston's a few feet behind her. "What's up?" She slides in between Charlie and me and gives us each a hug, her gold and silver bangles jingling on her wrist.

"Hey, big bro!" I say as I lean over to half hug Preston.

"Hey, Liv. Where's the waitress?" he asks, as he raises his head and tries to flag one down. "I need a drink. What do you want, Maria?"

"I would like that one, right over there." She smirks and discreetly points to a tan man in jeans and a polo.

"And she hasn't even started drinking yet!" Preston says, as he rolls his eyes. "How about a martini?"

"Yeah, I guess that'll do too." She shrugs and sits down. "It's pretty happening here. There are quite a few hotties tonight." This last part is directed at me, but I can see that Charlie overhears it and leans toward Preston to say something. Preston shakes his head.

I'm not one for meeting men at bars, but Maria's fine with it. In fact Maria doesn't mind meeting men at libraries, coffee shops, gas stations, salons—She seems to meet men everywhere she goes. Petite, blond, and with a smile that lights up an entire room, she's hard not to notice. In fact, it's not uncommon for drinks to regularly show up at our table throughout the evening. Tonight she looks spectacular in her skintight jeans, semisheer tank top, and adorable strappy heels with a zipper down the front.

"Check that one out," she whispers and nods toward the pool table. "He's a cutie. And look, his friend is even hotter."

I see the man she's checking out who is about to hit the cue ball. He is handsome, in a Maria sort of way. He has a shaved head, and his clothes are rather nondescript. Standing directly across from him is his friend. Not very tall and with dark and thinning hair, he is unconventionally attractive. The way he holds the cue, supporting it while gently guiding it in the right direction, makes me wonder how it would feel if he were holding me instead. He is wearing jeans that hug him in all the right places, held up by a silver-studded black belt. His white T-shirt is tucked in the front, not in the back. This friend, though, catches my eye for another reason. He is a celebrity.

"Maria! Do you know who that is?" I breathe. "It's Daniel Walker!" By now, Preston and Charlie notice who we're looking at. "I need to write this down." I yank my phone out of my purse and start to type.

"What are you doing, Liv?" Preston asks.

"It's Daniel Walker," Maria explains. "She needs to take notes in case one of her clients requests him," she says matter-of-factly and flashes him a big *duh* smile.

"You're really writing down what he's doing?" Preston squints his eyes and shakes his head at me. "Isn't that a little intrusive?"

Here we go again. When I left my steady, boring accounting job at William-Nelson to start my own business, Preston had a fit. He went on for literally forty-five minutes, without stopping for a breath, as to why it was a bad idea for me to start my own business, of all things, helping people meet celebrities. I wasn't surprised by this. He's always been very by-the-book. He graduated valedictorian from our high school, with honors as an undergraduate from Harvard, and from Wharton business school. He now works for Platinum Equity as an analyst. It's a wonder we've been so close all these years.

"No, Preston, it's not. He's in a public place, playing pool. It's not like I'm spying on him while he's taking a shower."

"But it's his private life, Liv," Preston argues. "If he wanted everyone to know about where he was, he would've called a press conference."

"If he doesn't want anyone to see him, he should remain in the privacy of his own home," I fight back. Maria is still watching Daniel Walker, and I can tell she's scheming.

"He comes here every week," Charlie interrupts. "He's a regular."

I look at Charlie and so does Preston. Why is he telling me this? He knows what I do for a living, and he's my brother's best friend. I would think, of all people, Charlie would loathe my career choice since he's a publicist and is all but friends with some of the same celebrities that I track. But he's never chided me about what I do. He's actually never said anything at all. So why he's suddenly offering his help, I'm not sure. Preston gives him a dirty look and then shakes his head. Charlie mouths *what?* back to him.

"Would you like me to follow him into the bathroom and ask him his underwear size? Would that help your clients?" Preston mocks me.

"I help them *meet* famous people, Pres, not buy them underwear."

"I just don't understand why you can't support yourself in another way. This is beneath you, Liv." Preston gives me a pitying look. "You're so smart. You should be doing something meaningful with your life. Something the whole world can know about."

"What she does makes people happy, Preston. There's nothing wrong with that. And the celebrities don't even know what's happening," Maria explains. She has always been supportive of my business. While working at an accounting firm she isn't able to gather much celebrity information, but she is helpful in another way. She is my human guinea pig.

Five years ago when I started my business, I had a lot of ideas as to how to meet celebrities, though no proof that they would work. It would have been foolish for me to test them out on my clients, so Maria cheerfully offered herself as a subject. Thanks to me, I think she's met more celebrities than all of the hosts of *Access Hollywood*, combined.

The first celebrity we tried to meet was Kyle Evans. He is more of a B-list celebrity, always playing the best friend in movies. I eagerly searched every tabloid and read hundreds of blogs looking for information about him, setting up resources for future searches. I had found online—on his fan club webpage, of all places—that he plays soccer every Sunday evening. By looking in the *Hollywood Hitlist*, a database that lists all Hollywood heavy-hitters agents, publicists, and home addresses, I discovered that he lives in Santa Monica (I now consider *Hitlist* my best friend. It costs a small fortune to gain access to but is well worth it). A few phone calls to some soccer-playing friends in Santa Monica informed me that there is a co-ed league that plays at one of the local private school soccer fields on Sunday nights, and Kyle Evans does indeed play on one of the teams.

So I had Maria join a team in that very same league. She started playing soccer every Sunday night, me on the bleachers loyally watching. *Loyally watching* Kyle play, that is. I studied his game technique and personality, calculating ways for Maria to get his attention when their two teams played each other. Five weeks later, the two teams were finally set for a match, and I had a plan formulated.

I had Maria wear a small amount of makeup and play with her hair down (which she fought me on, even though all women know men like girls with their hair down). The first half of the game she acted as if he wasn't there, playing her hardest as she had the previous weeks. But shortly after halftime, things changed. It was time for her to take control. She stuck near him, waiting for him to go for the ball. As soon as he did, as planned, she went in for the steal, the steal that was meant to fail, and did. Right as she was about to kick the ball, she "tripped" falling flat on her back by his feet. In the process of tripping "accidentally," she got her feet caught up in his.

Once she was down, the referee blew his whistle and everyone stopped. Kyle squatted beside her, sincerely concerned for her well-being, apologizing repeatedly. I was sitting on the bleachers secretly cheering. He then put his arm around her, scooped her up, and walked her off the field to the benches. My plan had worked. But it didn't stop there. As the two teams continued their game, he ran off to find her some ice. When he returned with it, Maria insisted that she was fine and that he should go back and play. Not only had my plan worked, but it had succeeded beyond expectations.

At the time, it seemed odd to me that it could be so easy to meet a celebrity and control the outcome. Maria has always said it's fate, that I'm meant to do what I do. I think I might agree.

"I'm skeptical," Preston says. "Your clients are so obsessed that they're happy when you get them in the same room as their idols."

"Wanna bet?" Maria seems to have taken over arguing for me. "We'll prove the power of what your sis does, right here, right now." *Oh, no. What does she have in mind*, I wonder. She turns to me and smiles. "Liv is going to make it so that Daniel Walker notices me." She pats me on the arm.

"You're on!" Preston takes his wallet out. "I'll bet you one hundred dollars that it doesn't work. You willing to take that bet, Liv?"

"Yes she is!" Maria answers for me, again.

I'm getting nervous about this experiment. "But guys, I don't have any information on him, other than that he plays pool at this bar." I'm not sure I can orchestrate an 'accidental' meeting without researching his background. I usually have at least a month to collect information and come up with a plan.

"I've got some information; I'll help you. Take the bet," Charlie says. Again, Preston shoots him a dirty look. "Sorry, man. But I think she's got a good thing going."

"Okay then," I smile, "you're on!"

Charlie starts to tell me everything he knows about Daniel. "He comes in every Friday to play pool. That guy with him? He's always here, almost nightly from what I hear. I think his name is Jamie. He's pretty popular with the girls, but Daniel seems to be a little reserved. I've only seen him leave with a girl once."

"Does he seem friendly? Have you ever seen him sign an autograph or allow a fan to take a picture with him?" I ask. What I'm asking is very important. A friendly celebrity requires a different type of plan than a surly one. They are harder to get to since they are nice to everyone; they assume everyone likes them. Great for a fan, but not so great for a fan who wants to appear not to be a fan.

"Yeah, he always signs autographs. Look, someone is getting one now." Charlie nods his head toward the poolroom area. Sure enough, two women in short skirts, low-cut tops, and smiles that stretch from ear to ear are giggling as Daniel enthusiastically scribbles something on some pieces of paper. He hands the two pieces of paper to the girls, and they almost knock him over as they lunge forward to give him a hug. Recovering quickly, he kindly puts his arms around their waists and smiles as though he greets everyone that way, even his housekeeper, giving them a big bear hug. The girls euphorically prance down the stairs, and Daniel casually turns back to finish his pool shot.

"I've never worked with him personally, but he has a reputation for being up for any charity event. Publicists love working with him. I don't think he has a girlfriend. He was last dating Kristen Landers, you know, from the TV show *Dark Dreams*. But she left him for some rocker." Charlie swirls his drink in his glass as he talks. "Ummm, that's all I can think of, unless you want to know what movies he's been in." He lifts his eyebrows at me.

"No, that's perfect. I think I can come up with something. I just need a minute." I try to drown out the thumping of AC/DC's "You Shook Me All Night Long" and come up with a plan.

Maria is bobbing her head and lightly shaking her shoulders to the music when I interrupt her. After I give her the details, she smiles and pulls out her compact to make sure she looks pretty.

"Okay, I'm ready." She beams.

Per my directions, she walks up to the pool table area and approaches the table. Daniel and his friend stop playing and look at her. She smiles and starts taking something out of her pocket. Daniel chuckles and, before Maria can say anything, grabs a napkin, signs it, and says something to her as he hands her the napkin.

"Ha! See! I told you it wouldn't work!" Preston stands up and does the touchdown dance. "Hand over the money, sis!"

"Wait," I insist. He stops dancing and watches.

Maria, now frowning, shakes her head and says something. She pulls a dollar out of her pocket, holds it up, and then puts it on the table. We see her mouth, "Next game," and she begins to walk back to us.

Daniel holds up his hand and speaks loud enough for Maria to hear him over the music. "Hey, we're just finishing this game. Why don't you play the next one with us?" he shouts, as he crumbles the napkin and throws it away. His friend chuckles and whispers something into a nearby girl's ear. She scoots closer to him, and he puts his arm around her.

Charlie looks at me and starts chuckling. Smiling at Preston, I shrug my shoulders and say, "See, I told you it would work." Preston mumbles inaudibly and takes out two fifty-dollar bills and throws them on the table. Now I jump up and do the touchdown dance.

"Dance all you want. I still think it's wrong." He takes a gulp of his drink.

Maria winks at me and heads back to play pool with her new friend. He welcomes her by giving her a cue stick and putting out his hand for her to shake.

The rest of the evening passes as Preston and Charlie debate over which sport requires more muscle: baseball or golf. I sit there waiting for Maria to return and save me from my brother and Charlie's male-centric discussion. I occasionally glance over at Maria and see that she's getting along well with Daniel. Really well. So well that what started as him helping her with her pool technique—standing beside her and guiding the cue stick—has evolved into his standing beside her with one arm around her waist and the other holding her drink.

I have to hand it to Maria. I may have the know-how when it comes to arranging "accidental" meetings, but she has the know-how when it comes to producing instant adoration. Finally, after an hour and a half, she stops by our table. She has a huge smile on her face.

"Wow! You just had to play one game to prove the point, Maria. You didn't need to spend all night with him," I tease.

"Yeah, about that," she giggles, "I'm going to head out with Dan. I'll call you tomorrow, and I'll see you all next week for my birthday." She gives me a big hug and heads back to Daniel who's waiting and watching nearby. Preston rolls his eyes and looks away, disappointed in me.

"I didn't plan for that," I sigh. "Poor guy. He's gonna fall in love with Maria, and she's never gonna call him again."

Charlie starts laughing. "Yeah, Liv, because I'm sure he's never done that to any girl."

Preston chuckles. "All right, I'm heading out. It's been fun. Next month let's meet up in my neck of the woods." He man hugs Charlie before leaning in to give me a hug. "I'm proud of how successful you've made your business, Liv. I just wish it were something a little less... gray."

"Thanks, Pres. I'm taking off too, as soon as I finish my drink." I smile, assuming Charlie will leave with Preston. Charlie turns to me. "It's okay, I'll be fine by myself," I assure him.

"I'll wait with you. Wouldn't want you to walk out by yourself." Charlie sits back down. Preston gives him a weird glance.

"See you, man." He pushes his way through the crowd and disappears.

"You really don't have to stay on my account. I'm sure I'll be fine. I'm parked just across the street," I insist.

"I don't mind at all." He smiles as he sets down his drink. "I figure I may have information you might be able to use for your business."

I look at him quizzically. I'm not sure why he is so willing to help when my brother has made it blatantly clear that he doesn't approve of my career choice. I think about Charlie's behavior throughout the night and how my brother kept looking at him. I don't know what's going on; regardless, I figure I can always use good information. Especially from a reliable source like Charlie.

"Well, if you really want to help." We finish our drinks as I ask a multitude of questions and Charlie answers them all as best he can. Once I've exhausted all questions, I put down my empty glass and start playing with the straw.

"Thanks, Charlie. This is exactly the kind of information I need to help me figure out the perfect circumstances for a meeting. You're the best!" I give Charlie a big hug and notice that he's blushing before he turns to push a chair out of our way. "Should we go?"

"After you." He smiles at me. "And here, call me when you're looking for any information about any other celebrities. I'll help however I can." He hands me his card with his new title, even though I have his number programmed in my phone, and then he steps aside to follow behind as I walk out of the bar.

CHAPTER

3

FIRST THING MONDAY MORNING, thinking of the information I learned from Charlie, I grab my Rolodex and flip frantically for Eva Howard. I take a deep breath and dial her cell number.

"Hello?" a woman barks into the phone.

"Hi, Eva, this is Olivia," I start. "I have some good news for you about Eric."

"Eric Cook?" she interrupts. "I was expecting your call."

"Well, he's back in town and—"

"I know, but the thing is that I really want to meet Nicholas Watson." She gets right to the point. "I've been waiting a long time for this," she impatiently rails into the phone.

"Oh, okay." I'm caught off guard. Last time we spoke, Eva had said Eric Cook had been her favorite celebrity for as long as she could remember. I clearly remember her listing every credit he has to his name, starting with the commercial he starred in when he was five years old. "So should I plan for two meetings then?"

"No, just the one." She rushes. "I've moved on from Eric. Now it's Nicholas."

"I'll get right on it," I quip back, brushing away the feeling of uncertainty that's rising in my stomach.

I've spoken with Eva numerous times over the past few months. She's been waiting on pins and needles for Eric to return to town. Even though she has shifted gears, I'm here to help her dreams come true. I jot down our appointment for next week in my calendar, assuring her I will have plenty of time to develop a good plan. I pull out some of my older case files and look for inspiration.

A few days later, at exactly three p.m., Becky and I sit in the lobby of a small, inconspicuous nail salon hidden among a bunch of cute little coffee shops and cafes on a quiet street on the west end of the valley. This is the salon where Robert Collins is a regular, and a few feet away from us sits his manicurist, happily filing some woman's toenails. I have booked an appointment with her for Becky and another manicurist for myself. Becky's been given strict orders not to mention Robert or any other celebrity. It is to look just like a regular morning out to get our nails done.

We take our seats, and the ladies get to work. As my hands are massaged and my cuticles are clipped, I observe everything around me. The bathroom door is on the left behind a curtain, co-ed. There are six mani-pedi stations in the salon and four chairs in the waiting area, one of them under a sign that reads, No Cell Phone Use, Please. The front window is small, and the view is obscured by a large flower arrangement on a little table. All of these details add up to one thing: I will need to be in the room when Becky meets Robert.

Becky and I make small talk to pass the time, to help her feel more comfortable in an environment I'm sure she's never been in before. The makeover she had earlier this week was a success. Her frizzy brown hair is now smooth and straight and has subtle blond highlights. Her new eyeshadow accents her brown eyes. Although her eyeliner is a little lopsided, it's still an improvement. Her lips are shaded a neutral pink, and the blush is applied evenly. With a few more weeks of practice, Becky will look as though she's been wearing makeup all her life. But most impressive is her clothes. Her True Religion jeans with rhinestones on the pockets are adorable and very age appropriate. They are matched with a fitted tank and a wraparound cardigan. Even the black ballet flats look effortless.

As we walk back to our cars, I tell Becky the plan. The most important part is that she *has* to get her nails done every single week at this same salon with the same lady. This will play the most crucial part in her meeting Robert Collins. Confident that Becky and Robert are off to a solid start, I head to the office.

As I unlock my office door, I take in the faint scent of the lilies that I have delivered weekly to help brighten up the space. A miniature smile creeps across my face, and I feel my shoulders loosen. I put my purse in one of the dark wooden cupboards that cover the entire wall, except for a large window, which overlooks the boulevard. The bottom half of the wall is lined with enclosed cupboards that have adorable sterling silver fleur-de-lis knobs. This is where I store my basic supplies.

I have everything from a variety of cell phones and walkie-talkies to books, briefcases, and even a small-dog carrier with a realistic-looking stuffed dog inside (don't ask). Above the closed shelving is a series of open shelves of varying sizes. This is where I have my coffee machine (which I only use for my clients and the occasional late night at the office), a few framed pictures of my friends, and a large display of business books and magazines, such as the *Economist*. I call it a display because these books are meant as a disguise for when the random stray person wanders by my office and my door happens to be open. They are also the only remnants I have of my previous job and serve as the

occasional reminder of how much happier I am doing what I now do—
making people happy rather than crunching numbers.

Finally, there is a row of enclosed shelving along the top of the
wall. These, but one, are empty. The cabinet farthest to the right is
filled with small mementos from my days as an active Brad Griffin fan.
I keep these nearby so I remember to put myself in my client's shoes.
There is one ticket stub, framed, from when I had a front-row seat at his
concert and he looked my way while singing "Waiting for the Day," an
autographed photo I won from a radio station, the first CD he released,
a rolled-up poster with a lip gloss stain that hung on my wall for many,
many years, as well as a few other smaller, less significant items that
round out my collection. The rest of my paraphernalia is safely stowed
away in a storage unit.

How I came upon this office can only be described as divine
intervention. After a few months of running my business from my
apartment and conducting meetings at client's homes, I quickly
realized that in order to manage my time wisely, I was going to have to
come up with a place to work where my clients could come to me.

I was driving home from my third successful arranged meeting,
when this building caught my eye. Although I drove down the street
regularly, I had never noticed it before. But as I sat at the stoplight,
something caused me to turn my head and look at this building. With its
brown, boxy exterior and Mediterranean window boxes, which brimmed
with marigolds, it appeared to me as elegant but plain.

Then I noticed a small, handwritten red-and-white For Rent sign
in an upper corner window. Of course I immediately pulled over and
punched the numbers into my cell phone. Five minutes later, I had
an appointment for the next day to see the tiny one-room office with
attached bathroom.

The lady on the phone explained to me that the office was originally
intended for the builder/owner's wife. Less than one year after it was
built, the owner discovered his wife was having an affair. Eager to get
rid of anything that reminded him of his wife, he told his realtor to
rent the office to the first person who came along, regardless of how
much rent they were willing to pay. When I saw it the next day with

its dark wood cabinets, bamboo hardwood floors, and lavender walls, I fell in love and signed the contract. Here I am five years later, still paying only five hundred dollars a month for a beautiful office in a prime part of town.

CHAPTER 4

IT'S BEEN A LONG DAY of research and meetings with clients, and I am really looking forward to going home. Maria's birthday is today, and since she says she'd much rather eat pie than cake any day, I'm making her favorite—pumpkin pie. While finding canned pumpkin in the middle of spring can be tricky, baking a pie is much easier than the German chocolate cake with fudgy filling she always makes for my birthday.

Normally I would just walk to the store a few blocks from my apartment, but my feet are killing me. I've been trying to break in these adorable new heels, though two hours into the day found myself wishing I had stashed an extra pair in my bag. With my feet hurting so bad I can barely walk, I stop at the Gelson's halfway between the office and home.

I pull into the parking lot and find a space amid all the Mercedes, BMWs and Lexuses. Once inside, I head for the canned-foods aisle. I know my way around this store pretty well since last year I arranged a meeting for a client here. Wandering up and down aisles, pretending to look for basic groceries twice a week for two months will give you some intimate knowledge about a store. Like hummus shipments come in on Tuesdays, though pita is fresh baked on Thursdays. And store-baked cookies are on sale every Friday after five (which led me to find out there's a 24 Hour Fitness down the street, as well, thankfully).

And my Gelson's undercover trips prompted another successful "accidental" meeting. While shopping for produce, my client "accidentally" knocked a couple of apples onto her idol's—Steve Cox—toes. She apologized profusely while Steve picked up the apples, and they had an in-depth conversation about what kinds of apples they most like. Random, but normal. It made my client very happy.

I scan the canned-foods aisle for pumpkin, remembering that it's usually in a weird place during the off-season. Rows and rows of cans are stacked before me. Canned beans, no...canned corn, no...canned peaches, no...canned tomatoes, no...canned sardines, ew, no. I scan the aisle for someone who works here. I see nothing but an empty shopping cart pushed up against one side of the shelving at the end of the aisle. A few feet from the shopping cart, I see a bright orange label that's wrapped around a can that is pushed a few inches back and high up on the top shelf. *Ooooh! That's got to be it.* I step closer and sure enough, it's the elusive canned pumpkin! I reach to grab it, and...I'm not even close. Again I scan the aisle for a worker to help me out, and there's no one.

I look around once more, this time for something to stand on so I can reach my prized pumpkin. I see the shopping cart again and realize it will make the perfect step stool. Surely whoever left it here won't mind if I borrow it for just a second. Pulling it closer, I prop my adorably clad foot right above the front wheel with the spike of my heel on the bar and pray the cart doesn't roll. I stretch my arm out as far as I can while balancing the other hand on the cart with just one finger. There it is—hiding beside a stack of canned sweet potatoes. My fingers grip the top edge of the can, and I'm about to carefully pull it down when—

SWOOSH...THWUMP!

The cart I am so precariously holding onto swings out and away from me, and my hand grabs clumsily for something, anything to hold onto. All it finds is the stack of canned sweet potatoes. My feet are swept out from underneath me as I go flying into the air, only to land on my behind, a shower of canned vegetables narrowly missing my head. I sit there for a moment in shock, trying to figure out what just happened.

"Oh crap!" a deep voice exclaims. "I am so sorry! Are you okay? I didn't see you there!"

I shake my head, lifting each limb, one at a time, to make sure I'm not hurt. Sitting there on the floor, I am dumbfounded. What just happened? Who is this jerk that just knocked me on my ass?

"I mean, I saw you...I just came around the corner so fast that I didn't see you were standing on my cart." *He sounds concerned.* "I'm so sorry. Really. Are you okay? Can I help you up?" He reaches out both of his arms and slowly, gently helps me to my feet. He doesn't let go once I am standing.

I try to brush myself off. Wait, why am I lopsided? I look down and...where is my shoe? "I think I'm okay," I breathe back at my attacker. He is still holding on to me. I wiggle my arms, and he loosens his grip.

"Are you sure you're okay?" he insists.

"I'm fine. It's just—" My shoe has to be around here somewhere. "Ummm, have you seen my shoe?"

He lets go of me, now that he's sure I'm not going to keel over. "Your what?" He squints his eyes and cocks his head.

Oh great. He thinks I've lost my mind. "My shoe." I point down to my bare foot and wiggle my brightly painted light blue toes. "It seems to have fallen off."

He starts to chuckle. "Oh, your shoe is missing! I thought maybe one of those cans hit you in the head and—"

We both start to laugh.

He looks through the pile of cans on the floor, under the lip of the shelf, and around his cart. I'm looking as well, and it occurs to me that I haven't seen the can of pumpkin either. I take a quick look up, and the pumpkin isn't there. Hmm. Missing shoes, disappearing pumpkins…I'm beginning to feel a little like Cinderella.

I must've let out an audible sigh because my attacker turns to me and puts his hand on my arm.

"Are you okay?" he asks.

And, for the first time, I look, actually *look*, at him. *Oh. My. God.*

"You're looking a little pale. Maybe you should sit back down." He tries to help me to the floor, but I shake my head and resist.

Standing right there in front of me, actually *holding* on to me, is Alexander Young. *The* Alexander Young who won a Golden Globe last year. *The* Alexander Young who has starred in at least two *good* movies per year for the last five years. *The* Alexander Young who was voted sexiest man on Earth in *People* magazine.

The same Alexander Young who just knocked me on my ass. And boy, is he handsome. Crap. I need to pull myself together. *He's just a regular guy*, I tell myself. *He's no different than you*, I force myself to think. *He's just a regular…*What am I doing? This is what I tell my clients to think all the time. I am not star-struck! I am Olivia—*helper* of the star-struck.

I clear my throat and manage to bring a smile back to my face. "I seem to have lost my canned pumpkin as well." I point to the top shelf.

"Is that what you were trying to get down?" He chuckles as he lets go of my arm again. "In the middle of May?"

Great. Now I look like a moron who can't keep her holidays straight. "Yeah, they seem to have put it out of the way."

"I guess not too many people are looking for pumpkin this time of year." Again, he holds back a chuckle.

"It's for my friend. I'm baking her favorite pie for her birthday," I find myself explaining without thinking.

"Ahhh. Well, we'd better find that pumpkin then." He turns to move his cart aside to keep looking. "Ha! I found them!" he exclaims.

I hobble over to his cart and there, as if in a window display, my beautiful shoe sits perfectly propped on the can of pumpkin. Alexander picks up them both. "Here they are."

Before I know what's happening, he is bending down and, ever so gently, wrapping his warm hand around my ankle. As I grab the shopping cart for balance, he carefully lifts my foot and slides it into the shoe and then places it back on the tiled floor. I catch myself being thankful that I got that pedicure with Becky and had time to shave my legs this morning. He stands back up and holds out the pumpkin for me to take. Then he holds out a hand.

"I'm Alexander. It's nice to meet you."

I take the pumpkin and place my hand in his. "I'm Olivia. Nice to meet you too." I take my hand back and tug on my blouse to discreetly keep it from revealing my lacking cleavage. "Thanks for your help," I say and head off down the aisle.

"I feel really bad," he calls after me.

I hear the whirring of the cart's wheels coming closer.

"Can I buy you a coffee or something?" He catches up to me. "I just feel so bad. Please. Let me make it up to you."

A coffee with The *Alexander Young? What my clients would give for this. Oh! My clients! I can't have coffee with* The *Alexander Young. That would be conflict of interest, wouldn't it?*

"No, really, I'm okay. That's not necessary." I politely shake my head at him.

"Please, I just, I feel so bad." His brow arches up as his kind eyes plead.

"I can't. I'm sorry." I turn and quickly head for the florist counter to pick up flowers for Maria.

I can't believe I just met *The* Alexander Young and he asked me to coffee, and I said no. Women pay me thousands of dollars for this exact experience. And here I am turning my back on it. But really…I couldn't. What if a client requests him and needs me to be there when they "accidently" meet? He would see me, and their meeting would be ruined. Or would it? I could advise my client remotely, so he wouldn't see me. Or maybe I could just "accidentally" bump into him and introduce my client as a friend. No, that wouldn't work. I have always vowed to keep myself out of the equation. It gets too complicated when I'm part of the experience. The experience is my client's, not mine. Right. It's settled. I did the right thing.

But why am I spending so much time thinking about this?

I ask the florist for a couple of pale yellow peonies, bright orange gerbera daisies, and a fragrant lily. She wraps them in flowered cellophane and hands them to me. Pumpkin and flowers in hand, I walk to the cashier, anxious to get home and out of this market.

I place the flowers and the pumpkin on the conveyer belt. The cashier rings them up and looks at me. I notice her eyes are growing in size.

"That's $25.04, Miss," she squeaks. *What is wrong with her?*

"So we meet again," I hear a sexy voice say.

Oh no. That's why she's acting so odd. He's back. I half look at *The* Alexander Young and offer him a tiny smile. "So we do."

"See, it's meant to be, you and me having coffee together." He is quite persistent.

The cashier looks at me, her eyes growing so large they may pop out of her head.

"I-I-I—" I can't seem to get out anything else.

"Just one cup." His elbows are leaning on the handle of his shopping cart, showing off his lean muscles. I remember reading that he just finished filming a movie where he plays a professional athlete of some sort.

I wonder what kind of coffee he drinks. Does he like the caramel macchiato like George Clooney? Or maybe he has his with almond milk and honey like Matthew McConaughey. Aargh! What am I doing! It doesn't matter how he takes his coffee! I've already decided. Having coffee with *The* Alexander Young would be an awful move for my career. No coffee. Case closed.

But look at those arms…

"Okay." *WHAT? I've lost all control over my mouth.* "But just one cup."

The cashier continues to look on, dumbfounded.

"Great." His pleading grin turns into an inviting smile. "There's a Coffee Commissary on Fairfax, near Melrose. How's tomorrow at six?"

The cashier's jaw drops.

"Tomorrow at six," I repeat, unsure of what I've just done. I pay for my pumpkin and flowers and try to keep my composure while walking out the door.

As soon as I get into my car I call Maria. It goes straight to voicemail. I leave her what's probably the strangest message I've ever left anyone.

"Hey, I was just at the store. I fell down, and I'm okay, but I have to tell you something. I'm not sure what I just did. Nothing like that, really, well maybe, I don't know. See you in a few hours."

CHAPTER
5

WHEN I ARRIVE HOME, I try to distract myself by baking the pie. The pie that started this whole thing. But details of what just happened keep creeping into my head. Small, annoying details, like those bright green eyes and incredibly strong arms.

First, I drop the entire egg—shell and all—into the pie filling and have to fish it out. Then I am about to dump half a teaspoon of allspice into the batter when I realize I've poured chili powder into the spoon instead. Finally, I get all the right ingredients into the pie shell and put the pie in the oven. Five minutes later, I realize that I never turned the oven on.

What is wrong with me? It's just coffee. Just two normal people drinking a normal everyday beverage.

He's just a regular guy. Ugh! There I go again! "I am not star-struck. I am NOT star-struck. I am NOT STAR-STRUCK!" I yell at the top of my lungs. A dog barks outside, and the man walking him glances up into my window. When he sees me screaming with my fists in the air, he quickly scurries away. Oops.

Know what? I don't even have to go tomorrow. I can just not show up. I'll never see him again and even if I do, he won't remember me.

I'm trying really hard to convince myself of this, but I know that last part isn't true. I did exactly what I have my clients do to get their favorite celebrities to remember them. I treated him normal. I acted as if I didn't know who he was. Then I turned him down.

Suddenly it occurs to me. Oh, geez. I created the perfect scenario to be intriguing and remembered without even trying. In fact, I was trying to do the complete opposite.

I open the cupboard below the microwave and pull out a bottle of wine. I'm definitely going to need wine tonight.

I get to Maria's at around seven with pie, flowers, and wine in hand. I can see through the window that her TV is on. I must be the first one here. I stand at her door with my hands full, trying to figure out how to ring the doorbell or knock, or even kick. I'm maneuvering the wine to under my chin and tapping the door with my elbow when Charlie runs up beside me.

"Hold on! I'll get that for you." He takes the wine from my neck and knocks on the door. I notice he brought a bottle as well. "Wow! That pie looks good." He leans over and takes a deep sniff.

"Thanks. It's straight out of the oven, still warm." I smile at him.

"You made it?" His smile grows bigger. "I'm surprised you were able to find pumpkin this time of year."

Maria opens the door and saves me from thoughts of pumpkin-finding, which come flooding back. She looks adorable as usual.

"Look at you, birthday girl!" Charlie says.

Maria holds her arms out and turns slowly, showing off her summery outfit. The dark purple fabric of her top hugs her body, accentuating her perfect little figure. A golden rope is woven through the collar and hangs around her neck, giving off an air of royalty. She has paired the top with some white chinos and gold and black stilettos.

"Thank you! I had to dress for the occasion. You only turn twenty-seven once." She looks at Charlie and her face lights up. "Oooh! You brought wine. Yay!" She grabs the wine bottles and trails off to look for a corkscrew.

Charlie holds open the door, gesturing for me to enter. "You look very nice tonight too, Olivia."

I look down at the outfit I changed into when I got home. Fitted jeans and a comfy strapless top with sequins scattered about, accentuating my less than voluptuous chest. Of course I put my adorable new shoes back on, even though I had to cover a toe with a band-aid. My outfit may not be as attention demanding as Maria's, but it's still nice to be noticed. She has always been quite the attention draw, which works well for me. The less I get, the easier it is for me to go unnoticed when I'm scoping out celebrities for my clients.

"Thanks," I say. Walking past Charlie, I catch a faint scent of cologne. I don't think I've ever known Charlie to wear cologne. Maybe he had a lunch date today. I'll have to ask him about that later.

I put the pie and flowers down on the counter, and then plop onto the couch and wait for Maria to finish pouring the wine, a task she insists on doing. Charlie sits down next to me.

While Maria's pouring, she says, "Sorry I couldn't answer your call, Liv. I was out buying myself a birthday present and didn't hear the phone ring." She hops over to us and hands both Charlie and me our wine glasses before heading back for her own. "Lisa had on a gorgeous bracelet that her boyfriend bought her. She said there was only one left, so I stopped at Bloomingdales to buy it for myself. I got the last one." As she sits on the sofa across from us and tosses her legs over the side, she holds up her wrist. A gold bracelet studded with small diamonds sparkles in the light.

"That *is* gorgeous!" I say.

"But enough about that." She takes a gulp of her wine. "What happened at the store? You weren't making much sense."

Just then Preston opens the door and walks in. "Birthday girl!" he shouts and pulls Maria off the couch to give her a big hug. He puts a vase full of flowers on a table and sits across from us. "What's up Charlie? Liv?" He nods at us.

"Olivia was about to tell us what happened to her at the store today," Maria chirps.

Great. I was planning on telling Maria about it in private, without any judgment from big brother. "It's nothing really, I just ran into someone at the store today."

"It didn't sound like nothing," she interrupts. "Your voice was all in a flurry, and you weren't making any sense. I figured you met some great guy."

Charlie turns and looks at me. So does Preston. I suddenly feel like the only witness in a pivotal court case. I need to change the subject quick. I'm not ready to have a civilized conversation about what happened. What can I say? Oh, I know! Charlie and his cologne!

"Speaking of meeting someone," I say as I poke Charlie in the shoulder, "why don't you tell us about this new girl?"

Preston quizzically looks at Charlie.

"What are you talking about?" Charlie looks at me, confused.

"Well, you're smelling awful nice tonight. You must've had a lunch date," I volunteer.

Charlie blushes. "No, no lunch date."

"Hmmmm. Do you have a crush on a coworker?" I look at Charlie questioningly. He shakes his head. "Or maybe you stopped by her place after work for—"

Maria is rolling her eyes at me. "Leave him alone, Liv. Why don't you tell us about *your* new love?"

"Yeah, Liv." Preston raises his eyebrows. "Why don't you tell us all about this new love?"

"It's not a new love." I defend myself. "It was just a… a…an interesting…experience." I tuck my dark hair behind my ear and pick at my fingernail.

Aw, hell. I may as well just tell them. They're not going to let it rest until I do. I take a few chugs of wine and…I tell them *everything*. From my aching feet, to the hidden pumpkin, to the cashier who watched on in awe. I don't leave out any details. I even find myself mentioning those muscular arms. I talk for twenty minutes without any interruptions, just silent stares.

When I'm done, I shrug my shoulders and add, "See, it's not a new love. It was just an experience."

Maria stares at me with her jaw slightly dropped. Charlie is staring at the table, his left hand ruffling his blond hair. Preston looks at me skeptically.

"So now you're *dating* celebrities?" Preston accuses.

"No, it's not a date," I assert firmly. "It's just coffee, and I don't even know if I'm going to show up."

"You want us to believe you didn't do this on purpose?" he adds.

"Of course I didn't do it on purpose. I was buying pumpkin."

"You were buying pumpkin at Gelson's. Everybody knows that's a celebrity hotspot," he cites.

"I was tired and my feet hurt," I remind him. "I just wanted to get home and make the pie."

"Liv, you get people to 'accidentally' meet for a living. Isn't that what you did with this guy?" Preston persists.

"Oh My God, he's right!" Maria gasps. "You did the Bump and Drop!"

I shoot her a *what the hell?* glare.

"I'm sorry, but you did." Maria puts down her empty wine glass and sits up. "You went to *his* store, walked down *his* aisle, and stood on *his* cart. Then you turned him down and made *him* chase after *you*. I'm sorry, but you did the Bump and Drop."

What *really* happened registers as I think back to three months ago when I arranged a meeting for a client, Brianna, and Paul Morgan (and his sexy Australian accent). I scoped out Paul for a month at the Gelson's in the Valley. Once I identified his shopping patterns, which was not that hard, the man is as predictable as Old Faithful (he shops for the same basics each week—canned fruit and organic cracker packs for his kids), I sent Brianna to buy a can of whatever was right next him. As he reached for a can, so did she, but hers "accidentally" fell on her foot. Paul took it to be his fault and ended up buying her an ice cream at the Rite Aid next door, where they chatted about his kids' favorite ice cream flavors. Thank goodness for chivalry.

Oh, geez. I *did* do the Bump and Drop! But not on purpose. I had no idea that *The* Alexander Young was shopping there or that he ever had, for that matter. I certainly didn't know the cart I balanced on was his. And I actually *did* need the pumpkin.

But did I turn him down knowing he would ask again? I did, after all, accept his invitation in the end. No. No! This is ridiculous. I didn't meet him on purpose, and I definitely didn't have him chase me on purpose. Really. I'm not even going to show up…I don't think.

Charlie pours more wine into his glass. "Anyone else?" He looks around at us. Preston and Maria ignore him and keep staring at me, Preston with an eyebrow raised. Maria is twirling her bracelet. Without saying a word, I hold out my glass, and Charlie fills it.

"I didn't mean to. I had no idea that's what I was doing," I confess. "I just wanted to get the pumpkin and get out, but when I got to the cashier something came over me."

"I know what came over you," Maria says. "Those arms came over you. Did you see them in *The Challenge*? He is hot!"

Thanks, Maria. That's not helping. "I'm not going to meet him anyway," I lie.

"Good," Preston says, "at least you're thinking clearly now."

"Yes, you are." Maria interrupts. "Why wouldn't you meet him?"

"It would be a conflict of interest. I can't mingle with the population I'm getting my clients to meet. That would muddy the waters."

"It would also provide information you couldn't get any other way," Charlie offers. "Really, you should just view this as career development."

"Right." Maria swings her hand as if to shoo away Charlie's comment. "Liv, he's hot. Do you have any idea how many women would love to meet him?"

We all look at Maria as if she's crazy.

"Right, okay, you do have an idea." She backtracks. "How can it hurt? It's just one date."

"One *coffee*," I correct. "It's not a date."

"Fine, if calling it 'coffee' makes you feel better."

I chew my bottom lip and look to Charlie and Preston. Charlie shrugs his shoulders, and Preston shakes his head.

"This is ridiculous." Preston starts his lecture. "Liv, you can't *date* this guy. You know how celebrities are. You'll fall for him, and next thing you know he'll be leaving you for Taylor Swift. And what's going to happen when your clients see pictures of you with him in the tabloids?"

Preston is right. One of my biggest selling points is that I understand how my clients feel. How could I understand them if I'm dating a celebrity? But Maria's right too. *The* Alexander Young *is* really hot. And why shouldn't I go out with him just once? It would be nice to see how celebrities live from up-close, instead of from across the Starbucks or down the supermarket aisle. While I'm at it, I can probably gain good insights or inside information for future clients, just like Charlie said.

"There aren't going to be any pictures of me. But I am gonna go." Again, I have lost all control over my mouth. I should probably get that checked out.

Preston rubs his hand across his forehead and looks to Charlie for support. "Come on, Charlie," he pleads, "you've gotta have some dirt on the guy. Tell Liv she's making a big mistake."

"Sorry, man." Charlie holds up a hand uselessly. "I've got nothing. The guy has only had one publicist his entire career. I don't know much about him. But give your sister a break. As much as you don't like her career choice, you still want her to be successful and having an in with a celebrity can help."

Preston seems to ponder this. "All right, Liv." He looks at me seriously. "Just don't go falling in love with the guy. It could never work out. Just get what you need from him and then get out."

That is all I'm doing, really, getting what I need to help my clients. And then I will happily go on with my noncelebrity dating life. Which happens to be nonexistent at the moment. Just one little coffee and I'm done.

I smile at Preston and know he cares. I can only hope that someday he sees the look on the face of one of my clients right after she meets her idol, and then maybe he will understand why I do what I do.

The doorbell rings. Maria shouts and jumps up to answer it. "Dinner's here!" The LAbite man hands her a bag from Cheesecake Factory, and she signs the bill. Even though it's her birthday, she insists on paying for dinner. The rest of the night goes smoothly, and *The Alexander Young* isn't brought up again anywhere but in my mind.

I'm having a hard time following the conversations and can't seem to work up an appetite for my chicken and shrimp. I keep thinking about what I'm going to wear to coffee tomorrow instead of joining in on the light-hearted debate over whether the Red Sox will ever again win the World Series.

But when it's time for pie, I find myself really, really enjoying that pumpkin.

CHAPTER

6

I'M DRIVING DOWN SANTA Monica Boulevard on the way to my office, a tea in one hand and the radio blaring my favorite jazz station. As I feel the sun beating through the windows onto my bare arms, I'm hoping my sleeveless white blouse doesn't leave tan lines. I pull into my office parking lot and drop a few coins into Harry's cup. He smiles and tells me to have a blessed day, just like he does each time I contribute to his food fund. I step out of the car and instantly wish I had opted to wear a pair of comfortable ballet flats instead of the kitten heels that I slipped on, in my rush out the door, not considering my sore toe. I smooth down my pink skirt and grab my work bag.

Once inside my building, I do a quick run-through in my head of the supplies I'm going to need for today's meeting: letters for Simone to carry to the post office, keys to my newly opened post office box (conveniently located very near John Cooper's box), extra stamps, a postcard, a small package for Simone to weigh, and a copy of *French Bulldogs of America* magazine to be strategically positioned to be "found" in the new post office box. I will also need a stack of envelopes for me to "address" while I'm standing at a nearby mailing counter, stealthily observing.

I don't normally work on Saturdays, but this client opportunity was just too good to pass up. The meeting's been scheduled for a couple of weeks, and I expect everything to go rather smoothly. Plus, it will help me keep my mind off of my date, er, *coffee* with *The* Alexander Young.

I step into the restroom to check my hair and lipstick before Simone arrives. Right there on my collar is a small dark spot. I must have spilled my tea! I pull a breezy, teal scarf out of my bag and instinctively wrap it around my neck. Happy with how I look, I head back to my desk and pull out today's plan to review while I munch on my cheese bagel. Not exactly the breakfast of champions, but it'll have to do.

Twenty minutes later, she arrives. Simone looks stunning. I find it hard to believe she is the same office drone who knocked on my door just eight weeks ago.

Simone found me through a short cryptic ad I ran in a local newspaper when I was trying new ways to find clients. It read: "Want to make your celebrity dreams come true?" After one week and infinite calls from creepy men asking for questionable services, I canceled the ad. Simone was the only client I gained from that important lesson in how *not* to word advertisements.

We scheduled our first meeting on a Monday evening after she finished work. She had shown up wearing brown tweed trousers with a loose matching jacket and a cream top. She had on tan closed-toe pumps, and her hair was pulled into a tight bun, accentuating her overly round glasses. But as soon as I saw her gorgeous, soft leather Fendi bag, I knew that she was going to be the perfect client. My first guess was that she worked in an office with a strict dress code; she later explained that she was a lawyer at a high-profile firm that was run by and largely employed men and to get respect in that environment, she had to act and somewhat look like her male counterparts.

So you can imagine the shock that is surging through me as I stand here with my office door open, staring at a beautiful, very feminine Simone. Her hair is a gorgeous shade of brown with subtle red highlights and flows down to her middle back in loose waves. Her glasses are gone, and her immaculately applied makeup brings out her pale blue eyes. She is wearing a silky pink camisole, obscured by a sheer cream blouse and perfectly fitting cream linen pants. Her feet are adorned (*wearing* is far too pedestrian a word for these shoes) with soft pink open-toed stilettos that look more like they are hugging her feet than supporting them. The only thing I recognize from our first meeting is her towering height.

"You look fabulous, Simone!" I praise.

"Thank you." She beams. "I'm so excited about today."

It takes me a moment to respond as I'm still taking in her whole presence. "It's going to go perfectly. And if it doesn't, then we know there's something seriously wrong with John Cooper." I motion at her, implying her looks, and then wave her into the room.

"I forgot you've only seen me in my work attire. This is more the *real* me." She follows.

"Well, you're beautiful. John isn't going to know what hit him." I open Simone's file as she eases into the overstuffed suede armchair across from my desk. "Let's go over this one more time before we leave."

We had discussed and even practiced, last time we got together, what she is supposed to say and do, and she took a copy of the plan with her; nevertheless, I go over everything, detail by detail, just to make sure. Once we are both confident she knows what to do, we pack up and zip over to the Culver City Post Office.

We arrive at the post office twenty minutes before John normally arrives. I enter alone, tuck the copy of *French Bulldogs of America* in the mailbox, and scan the area to make sure there aren't any last minute adjustments that need to be made to our plan. Noting that everything looks "business as usual," I walk back to the car to get Simone.

"I'm going to go in first and set up at a table to the left," I remind her. "One minute after I go in, you follow. You'll set up at the table to the right. Wait for my signal, then do like we planned. Okay?" I hand her the keys to the mailbox.

Simone takes a deep breath. "Okay, here we go." She smiles at me, and I leave the car as she checks her makeup in the visor mirror.

I enter the post office and set my envelopes down at a table to the left of the door. I pull a pen and a notebook out of my purse and slowly start addressing the envelopes. Almost exactly sixty seconds later, Simone breezes in. She sets up camp at the table to the right, across from the row of mailboxes. She sets down her package, pulls out stamps, and carefully starts affixing them to the envelopes I gave her. When she finishes, she pulls out the postcard and fishes around in her purse for a pen. Then she slowly, faux-thoughtfully, starts writing on the postcard.

I keep my side to the door so I can see when John enters, while Simone positions herself so she can see me out of the corner of her eye.

Finally, after several elderly residents enter the post office and make their way to the line at the counter, the door whooshes open and John struts through, jiggling his keys in his hand. I immediately drop my pen on the floor, my signal for Simone. She puts her pen into her purse, gathers her mail, and waltzes toward the boxes. Standing back up, I position myself so I can inconspicuously watch the entire meeting.

Simone is sliding her key into the lock as John steps up beside her where his box is, just two small boxes away. She turns the key and the door squeaks open.

He fingers his keys until he finds the right one.

She puts her hand inside the box and pulls out a few pieces of stray junk mail and the magazine.

He puts the key into the lock and whips open the door.

With too much to hold, she puts the previously addressed mail on the floor with the package addressed to a "friend" in Stamford, Connecticut, John's hometown, on top, making sure the delivery destination is visible.

He glances down at her mail, pauses for a moment, and then pulls out his mail.

She flips through the junk mail, stopping when she gets to the magazine.

He starts flipping through his mail.

She closes her box with one hand while holding the magazine in plain sight with the other. With no response from John, she "accidentally" drops her magazine.

Again he glances down, this time squinting.

Simone waits a few seconds to see if John will pick up her mail. When he doesn't, she bends down and casually scoops up everything. She starts flipping through all her mail now, looking for the postcard, our last attempt to get John's attention. And that's when it happens.

"You have a French bulldog," he states more than asks.

Simone looks at him as if puzzled, looks back down at the magazine, and then smiles the tiniest bit, as if to say, *oh, he must've seen my magazine.* She is good.

"Yes, two actually," she responds. "They're just the cutest little things."

"Aren't they? I have two myself. Pudding and Wilbur. They are a blast." He starts to pull out his wallet to show her pictures of his dogs.

I watch in amazement as I pretend to address more envelopes. I know John is quite the dog-person. I've read in numerous places that he always brings his pets with him on tour or onto sets of shows he's a guest on. So I was sure that he would comment on the magazine, as long as we got him to see it. I had no idea, though, the man carried pictures of his dogs in his wallet.

"This is them just last week at work with me." He holds up a picture for Simone to see. "And here they are on a gondola in Italy a few months ago." He holds up another picture.

"Oh! So cute! This one looks as if he's about to jump in the canal!" Simone giggles.

"Yeah, that one's Wilbur. He's quite the troublemaker. The poor gondolier fell in the canal trying to keep him in the boat." They both laugh. "He was not happy, and neither was Wilbur!"

Simone looks so graceful standing next to John. She, in an expensive designer outfit and he, in faded jeans and a worn T-shirt. Anyone who didn't know better would think she was the celebrity and he was the fan.

John pulls out another picture from his wallet. "Look at this one. This was taken when Wilbur was a puppy. He used to love to sit under the piano while I would play."

"Awww!" she sighs. "I remember when my little Lucy and Ricardo were tiny puppies. They grow so fast."

"They really do." He sighs and starts tucking his pictures back into his wallet. Then he looks at Simone. "I'm John, by the way."

"I'm Simone. It's nice to meet you." She smiles.

"You too. What dog parks do you take, was it Lucy and Ricardo, to?" he asks.

"We usually go to the Lake Hollywood Dog Park," she responds. I see she has done her homework.

"Oh, no, you've gotta try the Laurel Canyon Dog Park, on Mulholland." He points out the door. "It's way better. They have a section for big dogs and a separate one for smaller dogs. I just hate it when those huge pit bulls run around and scare the crap out of my two little ones."

"On Mullholland." She twists her lips and looks up, as if thinking.

"Yeah, especially on Tuesday evenings. There's a bunch of us with French bulldogs that meet there." He motions. "You should come sometime."

"Okay, I will." She smiles her charming smile.

John closes his mailbox and smiles at Simone. "It was nice talking with you."

"You too."

Mail in hand, he walks out the door, leaving Simone smiling and breathless.

CHAPTER

7

A LIGHT BREEZE FLUTTERS MY bedroom curtains as I stare at my towel-clad self in the mirror. Should I wear casual clothes? After all, it is just coffee. Or should I dress to impress? That is what I always tell my clients to do. But I'm not a client, I am just going to *coffee*, so I settle on a happy medium. I slip on my favorite dark jeans and pair them with a fitted black halter top that ties in a silky black ribbon around the back of my neck. I maneuver around the edge of my bed and into the bathroom, where I slather toothpaste onto my toothbrush. As I'm brushing my teeth, it dawns on me that not only am I going through my predate ritual, but I am incredibly nervous as I do.

It's just coffee, I tell myself as I open my makeup bag. I smear on sheer tinted moisturizer, as I recall the advice the esthetician I send my clients to always gives: Less is more. Next, I select a natural-looking blush; a soft cream and brown eyeshadow follows. I take a deep breath and steady my hand, which I'm trying not to notice is shaking, as I lean forward to draw eyeliner onto the edge of my lids and then apply mascara. Finally, lip primer, liner, and a dark mauve lipstick, highlighting the center of my lips with a little gloss. I smile at myself in the mirror, satisfied with my makeup. Then I quickly wipe off most of my lipstick when I remember I'm not going on a date. *Just prepare as if you were going to a meeting with a client*, I tell myself.

It's five, according to the clock on my nightstand, giving me at least another twenty-five minutes to finish getting ready. I untwist my hair from the rubber band I used to keep it up while I showered, and it falls, perfectly curled, loosely around my shoulders. Maria has always been jealous of my hair. She says it has that messy sexy look to it that only brunettes can get away with. If she were to do that to her blond hair, it would just look like blatant sex hair. I spray my messy sexy hair with hairspray to help it set and dance the two steps back to my bedroom.

Though I'm sure anyone in New York would consider my apartment positively enormous, it is rather small for Los Angeles. A little one bedroom in an adorable old two-story building that I affectionately nicknamed "piazza" after a brief obsession I had with Italy (I even took Italian classes, which ended in an embarrassing mis-conversation with a handsome young Italian at a bar).

The best part of the apartment is the living room. Since I'm on the second floor at the center of a U-shaped building, one wall is all windows. Standing in my living room, I can see the entire piazza before me, in all its flowering—tropical green, yellow, red, and purple—glory. Other than having a fishbowl effect at night, it is the most calming place I can think of, outside of Griffith Park.

I slide open my closet door and stare at the stacks of shoes, searching for the perfect pair. I ponder my black flats with gold chains and then contemplate a set of red pumps. I finally decide on some sexy, but not slutty, black and blue swirly heels.

I glance at the clock again, 5:20, and decide I should leave to scope out the area before *The* Alexander Young arrives.

I remind myself again that I am *not* arranging a meeting for a client, rather meeting someone for coffee. Then the truth abruptly dawns on me in all its ugly scariness: I am meeting *a man* for coffee. A very hot, and so far nice, man. And yes, this could actually be considered a date. And I have absolutely, positively, completely no control over how it's going to go. I can't remember the last time I was this nervous.

The Coffee Commissary parking lot is empty but for my car and two others. After all, who gets coffee at dinner time? I slowly pull down my visor and check myself in the mirror. I dab on a tiny bit of gloss and mash my lips together. I still have about ten minutes before *The* Alexander Young is due to arrive, and I assume he will be at least fifteen minutes late, as most celebrities always are. I switch the radio to a jazz station to help calm my nerves.

The dancing melodies bring me back to preteen nights spent sitting on our rear patio in a hammock, listening to my dad practicing in the garage with his band—the sound of the piano being played in an unpredictable but harmonious way. My hammock would swing back and forth as if keeping time with the soft brush of the drum, while the strong notes of the saxophone drifted up into the night sky.

I would beg my dad to take me along to the clubs where he occasionally played. Instead, he taught me how to play the piano like him, arguing that I would get far better memories that way than hanging around nightclubs. He was probably right. As a result, listening to jazz music instantly induces relaxation.

After one complete song, I turn off the radio, take a deep breath, and get out of the car. Looking at the other two cars in the parking lot, I wonder what kind of car *The* Alexander Young drives. Probably a Rolls-Royce, or a Ferrari, like Ashton Kutcher. There are a few people sitting outside the Coffee Commissary, one in a suit, one in jean shorts, and one with enough dirty clothes on that I think the shopping cart nearby is probably his home. None of them are wearing hats and glasses, so I'm feeling confident that I still have some time before my date, er, *friend* arrives. I slowly approach the door and tell myself once more, *It's just coffee.* But I no longer believe it.

I make my way up to the counter and am about to place my order for coffee when I hear someone approaching.

"Olivia?" a sexy voice asks.

I turn and see *The* Alexander Young standing beside me. No hat, no glasses. Nothing but pure, handsome, real Alexander Young. I smile at him, bigger than I intend to.

"I'm so glad you came." He leans forward and hugs me. I hug him back and realize I don't want to let go. He smells of fresh soap, Irish Spring. Then as he releases me he says, "I wasn't sure you were going to come. I thought maybe you just agreed so that I'd go away." He grins a small, shy grin.

"Of course I'm here!" I giggle and tuck my hair behind my ear. Ugh, I feel like I'm in high school again. I must get control of myself.

The barista stands watching us. "Did you want to order something?" she asks.

"Yes, I'll have black coffee, and—" He turns to me. "What can I get you?"

"I'll have a cappuccino," I blurt out. Cappuccino? I never get those!

"She'll have a cappuccino," he tells the barista. He opens his wallet to pay, and I reach for my purse, but he motions for me not to.

"I'm really glad you're here," he says again. "I felt so bad after I knocked you down. I just have to make it up to you."

So there it was. Not a date, just making it up to me. Whew.

"Plus, I couldn't pass on the opportunity to meet such a pretty woman for coffee."

Or maybe it's not just coffee.

He puts out a muscular arm to point me toward a nearby table. Again, I find myself getting lost in his handsome looks and forgetting my plan. How did I possibly think I would be able to pull this off? How did I ever think I'd be able to casually study him like a client and coherently gather information? The thick, dark hair that seductively curls at his forehead and neck, the muscular vein at his temple that reveals itself every time he smiles, those piercing green eyes that seem to see only me and nothing else. Yep, I'm screwed.

I follow his lead and take a seat.

"So how was the pie?" He rests his elbows on the arms of his chair, folding his hands together.

It takes me a moment to realize he is talking about the pumpkin pie. "It was good. We had a fun time."

"Black, cappuccino!" the barista impatiently calls from behind the counter.

"I'll be right back." He smoothly gets our drinks. As he returns to the table and holds out my cappuccino, he says, "Sugar?"

For just a moment I am frozen, my mind wanders to another place where *The* Alexander Young is calling *me* Sugar. I sit motionless and relish this thought.

"Do you take sugar or anything in your cappuccino?" he asks again.

I snap myself back to reality. *What do you put in cappuccino?* I wonder. "No thank you, this is fine." He sets my drink down and gets comfortable again. I pick my drink up and sniff, mostly because I can't think of a single thing to say to *The* Alexander Young. Argh! I need to get back to my usual confident self! *He is just a regular guy that happens to be in movies. He is just like me, just like the guy sitting at the table next to me. He has normal interests just like me.*

Wow. I need to remember to never tell a client to repeat to herself that her celebrity is normal. It's totally useless.

"Thanks again for meeting me. I hope this place wasn't too far out of your way." He takes a sip of his coffee. Funny thing, I'd never really watched anyone sip a drink before. Such a feminine word, yet when *The* Alexander Young sips, he does it in a most masculine way.

Okay, if I'm going to make it through this date with an ounce of dignity intact, I need to stop calling him *The* Alexander Young. Maybe *The* Most Handsome Man on the Planet or… no, really. From here on out, it's Alex.

He sets down his coffee and rests his elbows on the table, leaning in.

All right, Alexander it is.

"No, not far at all. I live in West Hollywood, just a few minutes away." Whew, an entire sentence that made sense. "Are you a regular here?"

"I have been recently. I'm working nearby on a project. I'm just coming from there, actually. It was a really busy day."

"What kind of project?" "Project" must be code for movie-that-you're-not-cool-enough-to-know-about.

"It's a new thing; I haven't really told many people about." He takes another amazing sip of his coffee. "A friend of mine from college is involved in this organization that works with teenage kids in Bolivia, helping them graduate from high school and really just making sure their basic needs are met. Unfortunately, the program ends once they graduate high school, and they're left with all these fantastic dreams, but no one to help them achieve them."

I am so taken aback by *The* Alexander, er, Alexander's story that I'm just staring at him, nodding my head every so often. I have completely forgotten about the cappuccino I'm holding.

"I'm sorry, I'm probably boring you," he interrupts himself.

"No!" I stop him, probably too enthusiastically. I smile and set down my drink. "Please go on; tell me more about the kids in Bolivia."

He smiles back, warmer than before, and continues. "After these kids finish high school, they don't know where to start to achieve their dreams. So this friend of mine, he had this idea that another organization should pick up where the first one leaves off. But he can't run it himself because he's busy working with the first organization. So I decided to run it."

I lean forward, pick up my drink, and take a sip. Shaking my head I say, "Wow. That's amazing."

"I mean, I'm not totally running it myself. I hired a partner to take care of the business side. I know what I want it to accomplish, but I needed someone to help with the actual footwork, to make sure the legalities are taken care of. Someone to visit Bolivia when I can't be there myself." He takes a gulp of his coffee. "But seriously, I must be boring you. Tell me about yourself. Are you a closet baker? Do you make any other pies besides pumpkin?"

We both chuckle. "Not a closet baker, unless you're referring to the size of my kitchen. I love to bake, but I don't have a lot of time with work." NO! Don't bring up work! What am I thinking? "And other stuff."

"Other stuff, huh?" There's that sexy vein and that smile again.

"Well, you know, all the charities that demand my time." I start giggling and hope that he senses, and appreciates, the sarcasm in my voice. I take another sip. Hmmm. This cappuccino is pretty good.

"Ah. I see." He shakes his head. "Picking on the do-gooder, are you?" He takes the last sip of his coffee.

Already? His coffee is already gone? I look into my cup and realize that I was so absorbed in what Alexander was saying that I, too, have nearly finished my drink. Is my date really going to end this soon?

He leans back in his chair again. "You still haven't told me anything about yourself, except that you're busy with work. What is it you do for work?"

Crap. Okay, take a deep breath, Olivia. People ask you this all the time, and you have a wonderful, vague answer. Let's dig into that brain of yours and recall that nonspecific, faithful answer.

"For work? Well, I, ummm—" *Okay. Here it goes.* "I'm a meeting consultant."

His eyebrows raise, encouraging me to continue.

"I help arrange meetings."

He furrows his eyebrows and tilts his head.

"When someone wants to meet with someone to discuss something, but they need help preparing for it and arranging it, they come to me. I help my clients portray themselves in the way they want to be seen, articulate the important points they want to get across in a subtle manner, and arrange the meeting in a way that's comfortable for them."

"So it turns out you're in the helping business after all."

"I guess that's true." I breathe a sigh of relief.

"Do you work for a big company?"

"No, I own my own business." I start getting nervous again.

"Really? What got you interested in…meetings?"

He really has no idea.

"Well, growing up I was pretty shy, and I felt like I lost out on a lot of opportunities because of it. I always had these great ideas that I really wanted to share but was never able to articulate. So I started studying other people and how they interacted, what made them different from me. Eventually I outgrew the shyness, but I never forgot how helpless it felt not to be able to communicate what I wanted and be heard. I kept meeting people who weren't sure how to go about creating opportunities and making their dreams come true, or where to even start, so I thought, why not create a service that helps people prepare and execute? And here I am, five years later."

"Wow. You must be a very perceptive person to be able to do that. And ambitious." He stares at me, completely focused on what I'm saying.

I realize that the butterflies in my stomach are gone and have been replaced by a horrible sinking feeling. I feel like I'm lying to Alexander. While everything I've said is technically true, I know that how he is interpreting what I've said couldn't be farther from the truth. Not only am I lying, but I'm actually impressing him with my story.

"So tell me one of your success stories. Tell me about the most amazing meeting you consulted on."

Before I can even begin to think about what I could possible say next, I am saved. Coincidentally, I am saved by some giggling girls who will probably, one day, be seeking my services, girls who Alexander and I didn't even notice enter the café. I wonder how long they've been standing there watching.

"Oh my gosh!" a blond girl with a thick layer of foundation slathered over pimples shrieks. "You're *that* guy!"

"No way!" The brunette with a short denim skirt and UGG boots squeals. "You are so hot!"

Alexander graciously smiles at the group of girls. "Hi, ladies. How are you?"

"His name is Alexander Young, you guys," the shortest and loudest of the group says to her friends. She turns to Alexander. "I can't believe you're right here in front of us! I loved *The Champion*. It made me cry, like, so many times." She rolls her eyes to emphasize how many times.

"Thank you. That means a lot to me," he responds, sounding sincere.

Alexander glances at me with a sheepish grin, his assumed cover blown.

I narrow my eyes at him, feigning the I-thought-you-looked-familiar look.

He shrugs ever so slightly, and I'm almost sure I sense a hint of apology as those mesmerizing eyes hold my gaze. As he turns back to the girls I realize at some point I spilled cappuccino on my top. But I can't put a scarf on now. I grab a napkin from the table and attempt to clean up while he's distracted. Thank goodness I'm wearing black.

The blond whispers something into the brunette's ear. The brunette nods and smiles.

"Umm, could we have your autograph?" the brunette asks.

"Of course you can." Alexander looks around for something to write on. The short one runs over to the counter and grabs a couple of napkins and then pulls a bright pink pen with a feathery ball on the end out of her purse. She hands them to Alexander.

"We have to take a picture of this and post it on Facebook," the blond demands.

"Oh my gosh, we do!" The brunette reaches into her purse and pulls out her Juicy Couture phone. It's completely covered in pink crystals.

"Will you take a picture with us?" the short one pleas.

Alexander finishes signing the three napkins and hands them to the girls. "Of course. Come on over here." He holds out his arms for the girls to scoot in.

The blond holds her phone out to me. "Will you take the picture for us?"

Alexander opens his mouth to say something, but before he has the chance, I take the phone from the girl. I hold it up to make sure I get everyone. "Okay, everyone scoot in real close," I order. The brunette shimmies into Alexander. "Okay, one, two, three, say cheese!"

The girls give wide-eyed smiles and then burst into giggles. Alexander looks to me again, lingering just a second longer than I'd expect. The girls take turns hugging him and saying thank you. They skip back to the counter to order their iced coffees amid hushed exclamations of "I can't believe we hugged him!" and "He is SOO nice!"

Once they are out of earshot, and we are both seated again, Alexander turns to me. "That was really nice of you, to take the picture for them," he says.

"I didn't mind at all," I explain. "It was kind of cute, actually." As cute as it was, the entire time I couldn't help but go over in my head what I would've told my clients to do if they were in the girls' position.

"Thanks, though," he insists. "I know a lot of actors find the interruptions annoying, but I've always thought that if it makes someone happy, why not?"

I smile inside. *He understands.* "I think that's a great way to look at it. I think most women can relate to a young girl meeting a guy who makes her heart beat fast. Remembering that helps you stay young."

He looks into his coffee cup and then glances at mine. "Appears we're out of coffee," he says as he leans forward onto the table again. "Since my day was so busy, I didn't have a chance to get any lunch, so I was thinking of grabbing dinner at this little place I know across town."

In an attempt to mask my disappointment that our date is ending so soon, I am about to thank him for the coffee and assure him that our incident at the grocery store was not a big deal. But before I string together the appropriate words, he looks up at me, and really looks me in the eyes this time. Not in the I'm-having-a-simple-conversation-with-you kind of way, but more of the I'm-about-to-say-something-I-really-want-you-to-hear kind of way. Taken aback by the sweetness those green eyes are radiating, I'm unable to say a word.

"I'd love it if you'd join me," he suggests. "I mean, if it's not interfering with your evening plans."

Interfering with my evening plans? The only plan I had for this evening was to call Maria and dissect my coffee date, moment by moment. Then Preston's words come sing-songing back into my head:

You know how celebrities are. You'll fall for him and next thing you know he'll be leaving you for Taylor Swift.

No, no, no! I push his words out of my head. Maria was right when she said Alexander is hot, and there isn't any reason that I shouldn't go on a date with a hot guy. I deserve it.

"I think I can make it," I reply.

I insist it's best for us to ride in our own cars and meet there, so he quickly jots down directions, in case I lose track of his car. As I'm following his silver Audi S5, a thought enters my head and I panic: What if I'm not dressed nice enough for where he's taking us? It's not like I'm going on a date with some guy I met at a local bar, this is Alexander Young. He's used to dating women who are covered from head to toe in Balenciaga and Stella McCartney. He's probably taking us to some fancy place like Il Cielo or Josie or Spago.

What was he wearing? How could I forget the way those bold muscles peeked out of his sexy short-sleeve button-up shirt and how the silky black color made his eyes look even greener. But his pants… Was he wearing jeans? Were they slacks? He was sitting most of the time, and I certainly hadn't been in the state of mind to notice his shoes when he was standing. Surely he wouldn't take me somewhere that I'd make a spectacle of us, would he?

Five minutes later his taillights brighten, and he pulls into a small, unsuspecting parking lot. We are nowhere near any restaurants I've ever heard of. *Oh no. He's taking me to one of those secret restaurants that only really important people can get into.*

He parks in a spot with a coin meter and waits for me to park next to him. *A secret fancy restaurant with coin-metered parking? Hmmm.*

I see him shuffling through the center console of his car before he gets out. I start digging in my purse for quarters, dimes, nickels. He jumps out of his car, walks over to my meter and starts putting in quarters. I get out of the car and walk up to him. I notice he's put in enough for two hours. My heart starts to flutter.

"Thanks." I point to the meter awkwardly.

"Please, it's the least I could do since you wouldn't let me drive you here." He starts putting coins into his meter. "But I understand.

You never know what kind of creep you might meet at Gelson's." He is chuckling under his breath now. I roll my eyes and shake my head playfully.

He steps back and holds his arm out for me to walk ahead of him toward the sidewalk. As I pass him, instead of waiting for me, he puts his hand on the small of my back. I silently pray that he can't feel my heart pounding.

"This is one of my favorite restaurants. I hope you like Italian," he says. "They have a great gnocchi menu. My favorite's the one with pine nuts."

"I love Italian. And it's really hard to find a good gnocchi." *A good gnocchi*? What am I thinking?

We approach a small, older building with a large picture window in the front. It is not at all the fancy restaurant I was expecting or fearing. It is an adorable family-run place with no more than ten tables inside. They are all taken but one. The walls are painted to look like an old, crumbling building with exposed brick. Ropes of garlic and antique pots and pans hang on hooks around the room. There are a few paintings of beautiful, old Italian buildings, one of them hanging a little crookedly.

As he opens the door for me and I step inside, I am hit with the most deliciously pungent waft of garlic, tomatoes, and bread. I feel as though I have been instantly transported to a small town in the hills of Italy. I take a deep breath and savor all the gastronomic smells.

I realize I must be drooling because Alexander says to me, "It's great, isn't it? Like a little piece of Italy right here in the middle of Los Angeles."

A small man with a tomato-stained apron and thick Italian accent walks up to us with his arms out. "Alexander! So good see you! We thought you had forgotten of us. We not see you in so long time!"

"Marco! You know I'd never forget my favorite restaurant! I was out of town for a few months."

I vaguely remember reading that he had just returned from somewhere exotic, filming his latest soon-to-be blockbuster.

Marco leans forward and embraces Alexander, who returns the gesture. "Ah, well, we so glad you come back!" He looks at me and smiles at Alexander. "And who is this beautiful lady you bring with you? Someone you meet while making your next movie?"

"This is Olivia." He clears his throat and looks at Marco. "We just met. At the grocery store."

"But of course! Food always brings happiness." He leans over to Alexander and says more quietly to him, winking, "And she looks much too nice to be in movies."

Marco grabs me gently by the shoulders and kisses the air on either sides of my cheeks. Alexander stands by watching, amused.

"Please, right this way." Marco bows and sways his arms toward the empty table in the corner of the restaurant. "I have best table in the house for you! Sophia! Please get Mr. Alexander and his friend some menus!"

We take our seats and a shorter, plump woman rushes over to us and hands us menus. She affectionately takes Alexander's head in her hands and says, "Alex, so good to see you." She kisses him on the forehead and scurries back to the kitchen.

I sit, smiling at Alexander, my eyebrows raised.

"I guess I come here pretty often," he admits.

The woman returns with a bottle of olive oil, some dark vinegar, and a plate heaping with flat bread that's chock-full of fresh herbs and spices. She disappears again.

"You've gotta try this, and you'll understand why." He pours a small amount of the oil on my bread plate and expertly splashes a few drops of the vinegar on top, then does the same to his plate. He holds up the basket for me to have my choice of bread. I pick one with rosemary and gently break it in half, then dip it in the swirl of fluids. I bite into it…and it's heaven. A perfect blend of salty, doughy, woodsy, tangy heaven. Alexander watches me in anticipation, his bread already swirled and ready to be eaten.

I subtly lick my lips to make sure no tiny, flavorful morsel has escaped. "That is delicious," I agree. He smiles and devours his piece.

"So you were out of town for a few months," I inquire. "Where did you go?"

He finishes chewing his bread. "I was filming a movie in Vienna. Such a beautiful place that you forget how cold it is."

I take another bite of bread, encouraging him to tell me more.

"We were filming in these woods that were pretty much in the middle of nowhere. So we had to stay in really old cabins that used stovepipes as heaters. We didn't have much contact with the real world for weeks. Every morning when I got up, it was just so quiet; the air was completely still. I would try to go for a walk and enjoy looking at the dry trees with little piles of snow on the branches. It was beautiful. I'd love to go back sometime when I'm not working."

I am so immersed in what he is saying I forget to chew. I never thought a celebrity would take the time to admire the filming location. I figured he'd be too busy getting massages and sleeping with costars.

He swirls his bread in the oil. "How about you? Do you like to travel? Does your job ever require it?"

My mind flashes back to three years ago when I thought it would be a good idea to travel to New York to arrange a meeting for a client who was in love with a celebrity who was doing a short stint on Broadway. Some of my contacts here in Los Angeles had been able to find out where he was staying and a few other basic facts, such as the gym he went to there and the descriptions of a few of his favorite restaurants. What they didn't mention was the enormous, extremely buff desk clerks at the gym whose job it was to escort gawkers out of the building, but that is only if you were able to actually crack the passionately guarded combination lock to the door. And as far as the restaurants, well let's just say there are a lot of "small family- owned bistros with doors that turn inside dining into outside dining on warm nights" that are in the "more ethnic parts of town."

Although I had flown to New York before my client so that I could verify my facts and come up with a plan, I quickly realized I had made a very arrogant mistake. After one week of hopelessly trying to catch a glimpse of a certain celebrity who'd be wearing the uniform long coat and hat on busy streets full of taxis that pick up men in long coats and hats—and trying to befriend a number of what I would describe as hostile, tight-lipped doormen—I decided to stick to the town I had grown up in and know better than any other place in the world, L.A.

"No, my work is locally driven. But I do love to travel. When I was graduating from high school, my parents sent my brother, Preston, and me to Europe for a month. It was amazing. We took the train along the Italian coast, going from one small fishing town to another. The colors of the buildings and how they sit there, almost perched on the ledges, is just breathtaking. In France we got to see the Eiffel Tower and wander from bistro to bistro, trying out our French to buy some food."

"So you're close with your family then?"

"Yes. I'm very close with my brother. We've always gotten along, but that trip really brought us even closer. We grew up relatively sheltered, so to go out and see the world together like that, and be forced to depend on each other, was the best thing my parents could have done to prepare us for life and what was to come."

"Do you see your parents often?"

I hesitate, not sure how to answer this. I don't want to lie, but it can be a heavy subject. I pause, trying to think of a way out of the conversation. But as I look up into those pressing green eyes, I feel the need to tell him. It's as if I've known him my whole life rather than a few hours. I take a sip of my water and wipe my hands on my napkin.

"My parents passed away a couple years after that." I try to give a half-hearted smile as I say it. The kind that relays, *Yes it sucks my parents are gone but it's been a while so please don't go all I-feel-so-sorry-for-you on me.*

"Oh," his eyes fall slightly, "I'm so sorry."

"It's been a while," I say. "And I've got Preston. And Maria and Charlie."

"Maria? The pumpkin girl! The one I should thank for bringing you into my path," he jokes.

"Yes, that's the one."

A young waitress approaches the table and asks if we are ready to order. Alexander politely asks for a few more minutes and hands me the menu that, up until now, has been sitting untouched between us. I glance at the rows of Italian names, before my eyes land on a long list of gnocchi dishes, clearly the restaurant's specialty. I read through them all, imagining which will not only taste the best but will also be the least likely to end up on my shirt or in my teeth. I decide on a dish that includes steamed veggies and a Gorgonzola cream sauce with the gnocchi. I notice that it takes Alexander no longer than twenty seconds to make his choice.

One hour, two dishes of delicious gnocchi, and lots of small talk later, two desserts are presented to our table. Sophia is carrying them. "We have some delicious sweets for you, on the house! I made them both myself, just for you two!" She beams proudly. "This is a piece of Nonna's torte, and here's some fresh strawberry gelato. Both are recipes that my grandmother passed on to me when I was little girl in Italy." We hear Marco yelling from the kitchen. She looks to the ceiling and throws her hands up, saying something to God in Italian, and scurries off again.

Alexander suggests sharing both desserts, and I gladly agree. I can't wait to tell Maria about this. Not only did I go for coffee with Alexander, but here I am *sharing* dessert with him after dinner at a restaurant *he* took *me* to. I am actually sitting here with him, instead of outside the window peeking in and jotting down for one of my clients that Alexander Young eats at this restaurant.

My clients. I feel a sudden heaviness come over me. I haven't thought about my clients once, haven't taken any mental notes or even asked questions that would supply useful information, and yet, my evening is about to end. I will never see him again, and the entire evening has been pointless.

But it doesn't feel pointless. In fact, I feel wonderful. I haven't had such a great time with anyone in a while. It occurs to me that even if I had gotten information, I wouldn't want to share it with my clients. The closer we get to the end of our evening, the more I want to keep every last minute of tonight all for myself.

By the time we are done, I am totally, completely stuffed and hoping that the top button of my jeans doesn't pop. When the bill comes, and I reach for my purse, Alexander playacts a look of being insulted until I fold my hands and let him pay. Marco and Sophia come out to hug and air-kiss us both goodbye as we are leaving.

Walking to the parking lot, I go as slowly as I can without being obvious, pretending to enjoy the cool night air. When we reach our cars, I turn to him. "I had a really great time. Thank you for dinner and the coffee." I can't stop smiling.

"I had a really good time too." He leans against his car. He doesn't seem to be in a hurry either. "I'm glad you showed up for the coffee." He pauses. "I'm even more glad you came to dinner with me. Maybe I can call you sometime?"

I'm unsure of what to say, afraid I will ruin the perfect evening. Alexander is quietly tapping his finger on his keys. Could he be nervous?

I feel so young, so clueless, like when I was in high school, standing in a parking lot with a boy I just met. "I'd like that." I automatically respond. I pull out my phone as he takes his phone out of his pocket. I notice he turns it on. I try to ignore the thought that he turned it off so he wouldn't be disturbed while at dinner with me; that is just too much for me to handle right now. I am still reeling from the shock that he is such a gentleman and that we have so much in common.

I tell him my number as he punches it into his phone, and then he tells me his as I do the same. We both put our phones away and are left standing there, facing each other in awkward silence.

"Great," he says smoothly, "we'll talk soon." Then he leans forward and gives me a big hug, not like the hugs he gave the girls in the coffee shop but a real hug with real emotion in it. I hold my breath in hopes that it will keep my nerves in check long enough for me to hug him back.

Then a wonderful thing happens. As he is pulling away from me, he turns his head in and kisses me on the cheek. The warmth of his lips, the smell of garlic and strawberries lingering…it is all so perfect.

I can't believe he just kissed me. A real kiss. On the cheek. Maybe he kisses everybody on the cheek, maybe that's his signature greeting or his way of saying goodbye. I try to think back to the restaurant. Did he air-kiss Marco or Sophia? I can't remember. But I know that if I stand here all night looking puzzled, he may never kiss me again.

We both get in our cars, and he waits for me to pull out of the parking lot before backing out of his space.

As I look in the rearview mirror and watch him drive away, I realize I have done exactly what Preston told me not to do. I have fallen for Alexander Young. And there is nothing in this world that could change that now. Not even Taylor Swift.

CHAPTER

8

I AWAKEN TO MY CELL PHONE vibrating on my nightstand. It's Maria. I groggily say hello and then glance at my clock and see it's two in the morning. She just got home from her date and heard the message that I left in my postdate bliss.

"He took you to dinner?" she squeals into the phone. "That's totally a date."

I can't help but let a huge smile creep across my face. "Yeah, it was. It was the best date I've ever been on." I tell her everything there could possibly be to tell, from the sexy way he held his water glass to the tiny bit of gelato that was stuck on his lower lip for a few seconds and how badly I wanted to lean across the table and wipe it off with my own lips. We talked for over an hour. Me retracing, and sometimes re-enacting, every part of the date, and Maria analyzing it all for me, telling me how sure she is that he's going to call and that I should continue to play hard to get. Because really, as Maria gently reminds me, I may be good at planning how to get attention from men for my clients, but when it comes to my personal life, I don't have the greatest track record. So I listen.

"He is just so sweet," I purr into the phone. "He's nothing like I imagined. Not at all like any celebrity I've ever done a meeting with."

"Of course he's not," she points out. "When you arrange a meeting, your feelings aren't involved. That's why it works. But *this* is the real thing for you. Think about it. The way you met, he could be some random finance guy or whatever. He just happens to be in movies and have every woman on this planet drooling over him on a daily basis. Including you."

"Am I an idiot?" I wonder aloud. "Am I in way over my head? I mean, it's only been one date and I'm already doing exactly what Preston warned me I would do."

"You're not an idiot," she reassures me. "You're listening to your gut. And we'll keep telling Preston and Charlie that you're in it for the career opportunities."

I tell her again how incredibly sweet and sexy Alexander is, and she gives me a brief recap on her date (handsome, smart, incredibly boring but a great kisser) before we call it a night.

I'm awoken four hours later. But this time it's not my phone. It's all the crazy thoughts whirring through my head of what a great time I had last night. For a moment I just lay in bed, rubbing my eyes, looking around the room for some sort of evidence that I really did go on a date with Alexander Young last night, that it wasn't a dream. Eventually I crawl out of bed, convinced that I could not have memories of such pristine details, like the way his skin smelled of oil and vinegar when we hugged or how warm his lips felt when he kissed me goodnight if it were a dream. I stuff my feet into cushy slippers and pat my way to the living room.

Once I light the fire under the kettle on the tiny stovetop for tea, I make my way to the living area and plop myself down on the overstuffed sofa and grab a tabloid off the antique table my grandma left me. I flip open to page twenty-three and stare at Brad Griffin and his normal wife. I actually read the article this time. "They are very excited," it says. "Expecting a boy," a mini-Brad, how cute. "Thrilled to be continuing this journey of life together," *blah blah blah*. The teapot whistles, and I toss the magazine at the armchair across the room.

As I pour the boiling water over a tea bag and into my cup, I notice the little red light on my answering machine is flashing. I must have missed the nagging signal when I got home last night in my state of elation. I hit play on the machine and listen for my message.

"Hey, Liv, it's Charlie. I wanted to see how your meeting went tonight, and uh, I…I guess that's it. Let's talk soon."

That's strange. Charlie never calls me. Preston probably put him up to it. *Nice attempt at spying on your little sister, Pres. You'll have to try a little harder than that.* I hit the delete button as I take the tea bag out of my cup and toss it in the trash.

I had planned a lazy day at home, just soaking in the warming sun on the patio and enjoying the piazza, but by the time I get out of the shower, I feel motivated and antsy. I need to do something. I start flipping through my mail, buying time until I think of something to do, when I come across an ad for a sale at Nordstrom's.

Maybe my little shopping excursion is encouraged by my desire to look good for Alexander on our next date, assuming there will be one. But really, what girl can't use a new outfit every now and then? I could easily go to the Nordstrom's down the street from me, but, instead, I decide to try the one in Hollywood. Although I do own a few designer outfits (it's a must when you occasionally have to go places that will only acknowledge your existence if you look like you belong), I know they will have higher-end brands there, and I want to get something that will really impress Alexander.

As soon as I enter the store, I know I made the right decision. The walls are splashed with bright blouses and skirts, and there are dozens of sexy little dresses. Before I can decide where to look first, a sales girl approaches me and asks what I'm looking for. When I tell her I'm not really sure, that I'm looking for a few new outfits that will make me look really good, I can see excitement growing in her eyes. She starts leading me around the store and pulling things off the racks and rambling on about what colors would look good on me and what length skirts would best show off my legs.

I am not shocked or even uncomfortable with any of this. I have accompanied several clients on their mini-wardrobe makeovers in the past. I just haven't ever had one myself, mostly because I like to think that I know how to pick clothes on my own. Before I turn down any of the sales girl's suggestions, I hear my voice in my head telling a client to "be open when it comes to clothing recommendations; many times what we would never pick off the rack ourselves is what will look best on us." So I keep my mouth shut and continue to follow the sales girl around like a lost puppy.

I eventually find myself in a changing room with more hangers and outfits than I know what to do with. And the sales girl is adding to my pile faster than I can dress and undress. Of course, the outfits that look best on me are the ones I never would have picked off the rack myself.

I settle on five outfits: a few casual, one for work, and one sexy little dress. I am so thrilled I pick one of the casuals—a pretty black skirt that swishes when I walk and a ragged tank top—to wear home. Of course I swing by the shoe department to buy an adorable pair of casual heels to go with the outfit and then the makeup counter, just because. Before I spend so much that I have to take a second job, I head home.

CHAPTER

9

THE TRAFFIC ON SUNSET IS horrible, as it normally is on the weekends. I'm waiting at the light on the corner of Sunset and Olive when I notice a large group of teenage girls ready to cross the street. I squint my eyes and try to read the names on their shirts, straining to remember if there is something going on that I should be checking out.

As the light turns green and the droves of girls continue to cross the street, one of them yells as loud as she can, "I love you, Christopher!" Then I remember: The latest boy band, the Next Generation, is in town for a show tonight. And right down the street is the Mondrian Hotel, well known for its celebrity clientele.

Although I'm not likely to get a request for a meeting with any of the boys in the band (only one is over eighteen), it's always good to keep a finger on the pulse of the future generation of celebrities and clients.

I quickly turn on the next street and pull into the valet entrance for the hotel (rule one: Act like you fit in). Thankful that I'm wearing my latest purchase and not my jeans and T-shirt (rule two: Look like you fit in), I wait for the valet to signal me forward.

There are girls everywhere. They are as young as eight—their moms trying to live vicariously through them, pulling them along—and as old as thirty. And every single one of them is anxiously, leaning over the barricades the police have set up, their eyes glued on those front doors of the hotel. Most of them have Next Generation concert shirts on. The valet guides me forward as I push away memories of a younger me, a teen tightly gripping a pen and concert program.

I hand him my keys and a tip, and then I confidently stride through the front doors, knowing exactly what those girls are thinking. *Who is she? How did she get in so easily? Why can't I do that?* In reality the only difference between them and me is a few years of observing celebrity and fan behavior.

There are more girls inside. But they are different. None of them have concert shirts on; most of them have long hair and meticulously applied makeup, and almost all of them look like they have enough confidence to fill an entire arena. *These* are the girls that know what I know. *These* are the girls who will experience the moment they've been dreaming of, though it might last only a moment, since there are so many girls and only four boy band members. The difference is the girls who are inside are calm. They give the impression that not only is it their *goal* to get to the guys, but that they *will* get to the guys. They dress the part. They think they are pretty, even if they aren't. If they are nervous, you could never tell.

I see one of the girls whisper something to another, and they both turn and look at me. I take this as my cue to head over to the lobby bar. I order a drink and take a seat on one of the white sofas, and then stare at my phone as if I'm waiting to meet someone and have important business at hand. Aside from the girls who fill the lobby, there are several muscular men, probably security guards, and a few in suits, probably agents or managers. Though it is relatively quiet, there is an undeniable energy pulsating through the room.

Suddenly, the elevator dings and everyone turns to see who it is. As if waiting for a dramatic pause, the doors hesitate, then slide open. A blond with straight, stringy hair in leather pants and a white T-shirt saunters out. It's Jared, the oldest member (and many would say the least popular) of Next Generation. He's with a young, nameless friend, who seems to be following him more than accompanying him, and a bodyguard. Many of the girls stand straighter, brush the hair off their shoulders, and a few even discreetly reapply lipstick.

One of the suit-wearing men greets him, and they fall into conversation. The whole time Jared is stealthily glancing around the room. The girls seem to be very aware of this. After a few moments, he claps Suit Man on the shoulder and starts heading for the door. As he passes a small group of people, a pretty girl turns her back to him while another girl in her group says something to him. He stops, shakes her hand, and looks at the girl with her back turned. Then, just as I would expect, he puts his hand on her shoulder and gently turns her around. They talk for a few minutes and then he motions to Suit Man. Suit Man nods, smiles, pulls something out of his pocket, hands it to the girl. Jared hugs her and Suit Man leads him away. As he leaves, I hear him say to her, "I'll see you after the show." The two girls give each other raised-eyebrow smiles.

As the doors whoosh open and Jared steps toward the white van that's waiting to whisk him off to the venue, I hear the mass of girls outside start to scream. Jared scribbles his autograph for the few concert-shirt–clad girls who were lucky enough to make it to this side of the barricade, raises his hand to greet the thousand or so onlookers, and then jumps in the van and is whisked away.

The girls, staring in disbelief at their illegible autographs, are left screaming hysterically. They are guided back to the other side of the barricades, and I watch as reality washes over one of them. She looks at the autograph, then at the girls in the hotel, then at her friend, who is still grinning helplessly. She smiles back at her friend, but I recognize a slight look of sadness in her eyes. I know exactly what she's thinking: *Is that it?*

This time the memory is too strong for me to dismiss. I had stood in front of a hotel, a lot like this one, fourteen years ago, pushed up against that same barricade, waiting anxiously for Brad Griffin. I had on my favorite concert shirt and was wearing a big button with Brad's face on it. Before his ride had arrived, he had come outside of the hotel to sign a few autographs. I waited patiently, trying to gather my nerve and calm my shaking, as he worked his way down the line of screaming fans.

When he got to me, he took my concert program and signed it. I took a deep breath and conjured up the courage to say, "It's so nice to finally meet you. I've been a fan for so long." At this he said, "Thank you" and finished signing. He glanced at me for a split second and said, "Nice to meet you too." Then he walked off to the next girl. I just stood there. Part of me was so thrilled that I met Brad Griffin and that he said it was nice to meet me, that he had held my program and actually *looked* at *me*. But another part of me was frozen and repeated over and over: *Is that it?*

Suddenly a rush of girls crowd into the lobby and everyone seems to go into simulated panic, bringing me back to the present. The security guards start jabbering into their headpieces, and Suit Man runs over to the lobby desk and shouts something at the poor lady behind the counter. She quickly picks up the phone and starts talking, but I am too far away to hear. Within minutes another five security guards show up, shoulders back, chins high, and proceed from group of girls to group of girls. I see the girls flash VIP passes, hotel keys, or money, and I know it's time for me to leave.

Later that night when I meet Maria for dinner, we are both giddy over my date with Alexander. Still wearing my new outfit, I feel a little overdressed for the local bar where we met. The other bar-goers must agree because they look at me like I just walked off a space ship, direct from Mars.

"You're glowing," Maria accuses.

"I am not." I defend myself. "I just got a new moisturizer today."

"No, it's definitely glow."

I try to hide my smile, but I can't. In fact, I don't think I've stopped smiling since I got home from the date. I think I even slept with a smile. "He's just so sweet. And handsome."

"Yeah, he sounds like it." She takes a bite of her burger. "Has he called yet?"

"No, of course not." I brush her off. *Hmmm. Should he have?*

"You're right. The good ones never call right away." She pauses and then gently asks, "You think he will, right?"

"I hope so." *He will call. Won't he? Or maybe...* "Should I call—"

"No!" She interrupts me before I can even finish asking the question. "You got him by playing hard to get. You have to keep it up."

"Really?" I plead. "But he's just so...handsome. And *dreamy.*"

"And that's exactly why you need to not call." She rests her elbows on the table as if to say, here we go again. "If you don't play hard to get, someone else will. And she'll get him."

I swish my straw around in my Diet Coke. I know she is right. It's exactly what I would tell my clients.

"So when do I get to meet him?" she asks.

"Maria, we've only been on one date. And I don't even know if *he* considered it a date."

"He asked you to join him for dinner, right?"

I nod.

"He paid for everything?"

Again, I agree.

"He kissed you goodnight?"

I start smiling.

"Then it was a date." She takes a fry from the basket between us. "How much do you like him?"

I'm not sure how to answer this, so I just blush.

"Oh? That much, huh?" She smiles and pats my hand. "It's okay to like him, you know. That doesn't mean Preston is right."

"I know." I dip a fry in ranch dressing. "It's just...he's in the *entertainment business.*"

Maria rolls her eyes.

"Think of all those entertainment guys we've met. They're all so—"

"Into themselves?" she finishes for me.

I nod and finish the last fry.

"But you said yourself, he doesn't act like a celebrity. They're not *all* like that," she continues.

"You're right. Charlie isn't like that."

Maria stops and looks at me, then opens her mouth to say something but thinks better of it and takes a bite of her burger instead. When she's done chewing, she stares at me hard and says, "That's a pretty harsh judgment coming from someone who works in the entertainment business herself."

"I do not," I declare.

"Olivia," she sighs, "you do. Maybe you're not in movies or you don't record songs, but celebrities are your business."

Celebrities may be my business, but I'm definitely not in the entertainment business. I'm in the service business. I am nothing like anyone I've ever met that's in the entertainment industry. I don't go partying every night; I don't worship celebrities; I'm not egotistical. And I don't associate only with others in my line of work. Although, I suppose, I am the *only* person who *is* in my line of work.

"Look," she tries to convince me, "you like him. He seems like a nice guy. Don't rule him out just because he's an actor."

"I know," I mumble. I take her advice. Not because it's good advice, but because I like him so much already. And I'm not sure I really have much of a choice.

CHAPTER
10

THE SUBMARINE SANDWICH IN my hand smells delicious. All I had for breakfast was a cup of coffee and a bowl of fruit from the coffee shop before I ran my regular research route. First I met with Frank, a doorman at a Hollywood hotel notorious for its celebrity clientele, and then with Sue, a nice lady who runs the organic juice shop and has a tendency to give way too much information. Finally, I swung by the newsstand where Maurice, its ancient owner, saves the best tabloids for me. I only have twenty minutes before my next client arrives so I barge into my office, toss my bag onto the floor, and grab the scribbled list of supplies off of my desk. Unwrapping my turkey and avocado sandwich, I head for the back of my office.

I open my storage cupboard and pull out a trendy Skater Girl duffle bag I bought at a secondhand store (I want it to look used for authenticity), and then I reach for the Pro-Tec skating helmet I bought at the same store. I move to the next cupboard and rifle through several different types of two-way radios, walkie-talkies, and cell phones. The one I'm looking for is sitting neatly wrapped at the end of the row: a small earpiece and microphone set that can link to a cell phone.

The meeting with Simone went just as planned. She was perfect. She did her homework, reviewed, and practiced our plan, and she was calm throughout the meeting. Today's client, Natalie, could be another story completely. I was hesitant to take her on because she is only sixteen years old, which is quite a bit younger than the women I normally work with, but her parents convinced me that Natalie is very mature and that they will take full responsibility if anything should go wrong. And they signed an extensive waiver.

We were supposed to execute her meeting in another three weeks, but her parents decided to send her to France to stay with an aunt for the summer. She leaves in three days, and, of course, her celebrity, Zach Bryan, is leaving in August for a leg of his world tour. So the only possible time to arrange the "accidental" meeting is this afternoon. I was really hoping for the extra weeks to get her ready. She doesn't need any sort of physical makeover, but she is a teenager, and teenagers just tend to be unpredictable. And I'm not sure she's emotionally ready to meet her idol. Not to mention he is practically a teenager himself, only eighteen, making the whole meeting that much more unpredictable.

So here I am, preparing a hormone-filled teenager to meet her hormone-filled teen idol. I'm starting to wonder what on earth I was thinking when I agreed to this, though I really do know what I was thinking. I was thinking Natalie reminds me of myself when I was standing outside Brad Griffin's hotel. She showed up to my office wearing a T-shirt from her idol's most recent tour and shared that her bedroom wall is covered with posters of Zach Bryan and that her life-long dream is to marry him.

After several extended telephone conversations, which consisted mainly of Natalie talking about how dreamy Zach's hair is and how hot he looks driving his convertible, I was able to pry out of her that she has a hobby. That hobby is skateboarding. This came as wonderful news since Zach Bryan is a notorious skater. Even better, it didn't take much research to find out that Zach spends every evening at his local skate park. In fact, I just called the park, and the information was almost offered to me. Young and new celebrities are so eager for the spotlight that it's altogether too easy to get information on their daily whereabouts. It almost makes me feel guilty for charging to arrange a meeting.

In doing my research, I found that all of Zach's girlfriends have been skaters themselves or, at least, were pictured skating with him. Since Natalie is pretty and already knows how to skate—a detail I would have verified more thoroughly given the time—we have overcome our biggest obstacle. We just need to be able to get her close enough to Zach that he notices her. Then she will compliment him on one of his moves. Rumored to be rather overconfident, this will hopefully get him talking to her. I will be listening in the whole time and offering guidance, if necessary, on the two-way walkie-talkie. Normally I would have done several practice runs and role-play, simulating various scenarios, but under the present circumstance, we will have only a few hours in my office to prepare before the meeting.

I am very nervous about this one, but I can't let it show. Part of my job is to be calm while my client is a nervous wreck.

I squeeze the earpiece into the hole that I cut out of the inside of the helmet and attach the mouthpiece to the opposite inside edge. I turn it on and a tap-tap, coming through to my phone, confirms that it's working. Confident that I'm prepared on my end, I slide into my Herman Miller chair, toss off my shoes, and run my toes through the purple shag carpet under my desk. The only benefit of working with a teenager is that I get to wear comfortable jeans and a trendy and soft scoop-neck top. Knowing Natalie will be arriving any second, I devour the rest of my sandwich.

As I slurp up the last of my Diet Coke, there is a loud, clumsy knock at my door. Natalie and her mom are here. I let them in, and Natalie takes a seat while her mother lingers by the door.

"Hi Natalie, hi Susan," I greet them. "Are you excited about meeting Zach today?"

"Yeah," Natalie squeaks.

Uh-oh, what happened to the Natalie who goes on for hours about how hot Zach is?

"She seems a bit nervous," her mother explains. "I tried my best to get her to eat today, but she hasn't quite been herself."

Natalie sits there, chewing one of her painted black fingernails.

"Natalie, are you ready for this?" I ask as I walk over and sit on the edge of the desk in front of her. "We can always push this back. We can do it when he gets back from Asia."

Natalie stops, slowly looks up at me, eyes widening, and I can see she's about to cry.

"She's just kidding," her mother jumps in. Natalie looks at her. "You're still meeting him today. Olivia was just trying to cheer you up by making a joke. Weren't you, Olivia?"

I want to say, *No, I think this is a bad idea. I think we need more time to plan so this can go as close to perfect as possible.* But instead, I say, "Of course I'm joking. This is going to be great. *You* are going to be great." I smile calmly. "We are going to go skating with Zach Bryan, and it's going to be wonderful."

"Okay, see sweetie?" Susan rubs Natalie's arm. "I'm going to go now and let you and Olivia get ready. Zach is going to fall in love the instant he sees you. It will all be wonderful." She leans down and kisses Natalie on the forehead and leaves.

Zach is going to fall in love the instant he sees you? How am I supposed to deliver that? Looking at Natalie, I'm thinking we'll be lucky if she doesn't pass out as soon as we see him.

"Do you want some water, Natalie?" I ask. She shakes her head. "How about a snack? You need to eat something before we go." She looks up at me and gives me a half-hearted smile. I pull open a drawer and hand her a chocolate chip granola bar. I always have granola bars on hand. It's not uncommon for my clients to show up hungry, their nerves having gotten the best of their stomachs.

She takes the bar and slowly unwraps it.

"As soon as you finish eating it, you'll feel much better," I tell her. She smiles a little as she starts to munch. "You really have nothing to be nervous about. I mean, how long have you been skating? You said six years, right?"

She nods and continues to munch.

"So you've been skating longer than Zach's been performing. And you're meeting him while doing something you like to do and are comfortable doing. You know exactly what is going on. You're going to meet Zach on your terms. He's the one who should be nervous. He has no idea that he's about to meet a beautiful, smart, young woman."

She is nodding more now and taking bigger bites of the granola bar.

I'm giving a version of the same speech I've given for five years. But somehow, today, even I'm having a hard time believing it. Maybe it's because I can't stop thinking about Alexander and how nervous I was on the way to coffee. And dinner.

I've got to find a way to use this to my advantage.

"We are in charge here. We are prepared," I go on. "We are going to knock his socks off!"

Natalie is now vigorously nodding and swallowing the last piece of the bar.

"YES!" she cries. "We are going to knock his socks off!"

"Okay, then." I take the wrapper from her. "Let's do some role-playing and go meet Zach!"

Natalie stands up and brushes the crumbs off her pink and gray camouflage cargo capris. She looks rather adorable in her skating garb. She has on a dark gray tank top with a pink faded T-shirt that has been shredded into a loose tank top. Her bright pink Converse high-tops bring out the neon pink graphics on the skateboard she has propped against the chair. She has tamed her curly hair into two low, long braids that will fit snugly under her helmet. At least we have her looks going for us.

"The first thing that you need to remember is that Zach is a regular person, just like you. He just happens to be in movies." As I say this, I remember telling myself the same thing when I was nervous about talking with Alexander and how little it worked to calm me. I quickly push him out of my head and come up with a more compelling argument. "He does the same kind of stuff you do every day, and he talks the same way every other teenager talks. You just need to be yourself and act as you would around your friends, and everything will fall into place. Okay?"

Everything I'm saying to Natalie, I said and did when I was out with Alexander. Is that why Alexander wanted to see me again? Maybe I *was* subconsciously trying to get his attention...I must bring the focus back to my client.

"Okay." She smiles at me. "I just need to be myself."

"Let's talk about how you're going to get his attention."

We go over the plan, detail by detail. Natalie stops me a few times to ask simple questions or to tell me how she thinks Zach will react, but, for the most part, she sounds semiconfident and excited about meeting him. She tries on the helmet, and I feed her a few lines, just in case, and she practices repeating them in a natural voice. This is a tactic I use when I feel my client is extra-nervous. Usually just knowing that I am there on a walkie-talkie to help her out is enough to get her through. But today, I am not sure we won't be needing some real-time guidance.

"Let's try some role-playing," I say to her. "I'll be Zach. I want you to follow the plan we just talked about. Remember, he's just a regular guy. Just like all the guys you go to school with."

She gives me a look that reminds me how boys were in high school, and I realize that was probably not the best thing to say to give her confidence.

"Actually, he's older than the boys you go to school with. So think about a nice, mature young guy."

"Like Jake, my next-door neighbor," she suggests. "He's really sweet. He always asks if my grandma needs help down the front stairs and how school's going for me."

"Great! That's what I want you to think of when you're with Zach. Talk to him just like you would talk to Jake. Okay, so now I'm Zach, and here I come to the top of the ramp next to you. Go ahead and talk to me like I'm Jake."

She takes a deep breath and closes her eyes for a few seconds. "Hey, that was a really cool 360 you did."

"Thanks," I say in my fake teenage boy voice. Natalie giggles. Then…

She just stands there looking at me. I can tell she's trying to come up with something to say but can't.

"Remember, it's just like talking to Jake," I encourage her. Then I add, in my fake teenage boy voice, "I've been working on that move a while."

"Well, it was really cool," she says and then looks at me and shrugs. "I'm sorry. I've never really been good at talking to boys. I mean, I usually just tell Jake that school is good and then go inside." She flops onto the chair. "I'm never going to be able to pull this off. Zach is going to think I'm a mumbling idiot! He'll never think I'm as cool as those girls who hang around him in pictures."

Me. She's talking about me. Not that I've ever been in a picture with Zack Bryan, but now I'm that girl that would or *could* be in a picture with Alexander Young. I quickly push the thought out of my head and focus on the task at hand.

Teenage unpredictability is already rearing its ugly head. "Look, Natalie, what you're feeling is totally normal. All the women I work with feel it at some point. It's just a matter of recognizing that you're nervous and moving on. The more you dwell on what you believe is wrong with you, the more nervous you'll become."

"Really? Everyone feels this way?" she asks.

"Yes, everyone. Even the women that run big businesses get nervous when they're about to meet someone important to them. Once you're okay with being nervous, we can move on to how to deal with it. Like having a back-up plan."

"Like Cyrano de Bergerac!" she enthuses.

I pause a moment, surprised at how well read Natalie is. I begin to understand why her mom wants her to go to France for the summer— it's a learning opportunity, not a ploy to send her away.

"Exactly!" I rejoice with her. "Okay, so let's try it again and then get going."

We role-play a few more times with me giving her best-case scenarios rather than what will most likely happen in reality. At this point, the best thing I can do is to help boost her self-confidence and hope everything else plays out in her favor. I give her one more pep talk before we grab our stuff and head out to the car.

During most of the drive to the skate park, Natalie is talking about how gorgeous Zach is and telling me about his past movies and his last concert, giving the kind of details only a teenage girl can. When we arrive at the parking lot, I pull out some lip gloss and hand it to Natalie. "Here. Guys love it when girls have gloss on." She looks at me puzzled. I throw my hands up in the air. "I don't know why, but I always feel like it helps."

Did I have lip gloss on when I met Alexander at the grocery store?

She takes it and slathers some on, and I tell her to mush her lips together. "Okay. I can do this. I think I'm ready." Then she slowly turns her head to me and calmly says, "Oh My God, I'm going to meet Zach Bryan." Then she smiles a beautiful, youthful smile.

"Smile at Zach like that, Natalie," I encourage her, "and you'll have his attention."

I point to the grassy field overlooking the skate park where I'll be monitoring from. Then we double check to make sure the headpiece is working. Once we are confident that everything is ready, I leave the car and head to my position with a paperback novel in hand. I get to my spot, call her on her cell phone, and she leaves the car with all her gear. I watch her walk across the parking lot and start making small talk to distract her. I really want this to work out, not only because she's my client, but because I know it's the kind of thing that could build someone like Natalie's confidence.

She is telling me about her trip to France when I spot Zach Bryan. He is in the seating area, right by the entrance, talking to another boy (man?) and spinning the tires on his skateboard.

Whether it's Natalie's nerves or the fact that she's so caught up talking about her upcoming trip to France, she doesn't notice Zach as she walks right past him. He, however, does notice her. He stops talking just long enough to watch her walk by and then turns back to his friend to continue his conversation. I tell her to find a seat and get her helmet out. She does. Then I distract her with more questions about France and school as I watch Zach enter the skating area.

"Okay, Natalie, we need to hang up now so you can go out there and do your thing. Remember, I'll be listening in through your helmet-piece if you need me."

She hangs up the phone, puts on her helmet, and cautiously, slowly, meanders toward the entrance. I dial into the helmet earpiece and watch as she casually reaches up, pretending to adjust the helmet, ever so subtly switching on the earpiece.

"Good luck," I whisper into the phone. I hear in return the humming of the skateboard wheels and her soft breath.

She starts out slowly, first skating in small zigzags, then getting more and more bold as she warms up. After a few minutes, she skates toward the ramps and then down them as I watch in amazement. She is an inspiring skater. She glides up one side of the ramp and into the air, where she seems to hang suspended before smoothly returning to the ground and whirring back in the opposite direction, her long braided hair following.

Every time she takes flight from a ramp, she hits a new pose, each just as graceful as the one before. Watching her move throughout the park is like watching a perfectly choreographed dance; pausing here and there only to catch her breath, she's off, making skating look like an art. As I'm watching her, it occurs to me that perhaps her love for skating isn't driven by Zach, but her love for Zach is driven by skating.

Then I start to wonder—Is that why I like Alexander? Because he's the Brad Griffin I never got? Because he represents all the celebrities that we noncelebrities can never have?

Concentrate, Olivia. You can think about Alexander all you want later. I push the thought out of my head and refocus on Natalie.

I am not the only one who notices Natalie's talent. Nearly every being in the park has watched her, in awe, for at least a moment, even Zach. Although he was on the other side of the park when she started skating, he is now slowly working his way toward where she is, though I'm not sure she realizes. She seems lost in her own world of sliding and suspending, sliding and suspending.

"Okay, Natalie," I gently nudge. "He's coming toward you."

She skates to a stop at the top of a nearby ramp, kicks the end of her board, and it magically lands in here arms. She looks around her. I assume she is scoping out the situation to see how she can get closer to Zach. She is looking to the bottom of the ramp next to her, where Zach is doing some fancy move with the skateboard spinning under his toe while his leg is in the air, leaving him hovering. Suddenly, he changes direction and skates up Natalie's ramp. I suck in my breath and can hear that Natalie has too.

"Nice Impossible." She nods to him.

I exhale. I have no idea what she's talking about, but Zach seems to.

"Thanks, I've been trying to perfect it for my next movie," he boasts. "I see you had some pretty cool moves out there too."

I hold in a chuckle. That's one predictable thing about celebrity teenage boys—they're rarely modest. Then I notice that Natalie hasn't responded to him. I begin to panic, has my headset broken? Did I lose the connection? I hear a very slight, shallow breathing and the panic disappears. My connection is still there. But Natalie! She's not saying anything! The panic begins to return. I give her another few seconds to compose herself. I don't want her to think I don't have faith in her; she needs all the confidence-boosting she can get.

Still nothing.

I have no choice but to pull a Cyrano de Bergerac.

"Okay, take a deep breath," I calmly lull into the phone. "First you need to give him that beautiful smile of yours." I can see that she does. "Now just repeat after me, 'How long have you been working on that move?"

She pauses, then repeats what I said word for word, inflection for inflection.

"About two months," he continues. "I can't seem to perfect the landing though. The first part isn't that hard when you know how to do some other moves, like the ones you were doing earlier. But that landing, there's something weird about it if you don't get the momentum right." He shakes his head.

"It looks really hard," I direct into the phone.

She repeats my line with more confidence, adding her own personality to the delivery.

"You've never tried it?" He looks surprised.

I can't answer for her because I don't know if she has.

"No, I've wanted to, but I've only seen Rodney Mullen do one on TV," Natalie admits on her own.

"Yeah, it's hard to replicate stuff you haven't seen in person. They hired a skating coach for me, and that's where I learned." He picks up his skateboard, spinning it on its edge with one hand, the other hand at his side.

"That's gotta be cool, to have someone who can show you all the moves you want to learn." She spins a wheel of her skateboard as she talks.

"Yeah, it is." He tucks a straggly piece of blond hair into his helmet above his eye. "Do you want me to show you how to do it?"

"Yeah!" Natalie smiles at him again. "That would be awesome."

Zach drops an end of his skateboard onto the ground, still holding the other end with his toe. He pulls at his tight gray jeans, just enough so that they don't fall off but we can still see his black-and-white plaid boxers underneath. He moves down the ramp. Natalie tosses her skateboard to the ground, jumps on, and follows after him.

CHAPTER
11

A LEXANDER CALLS THAT WEDNESDAY, exactly three days, fourteen hours, and twenty-three minutes after we met at the coffee shop. Not that I'm counting.

I'm sitting at my desk, reading through a file for a potential client when I hear my cell phone ring.

"Olivia!" my heart immediately starts beating faster. After a few moments of silence, the deep, sexy voice continues. "It's me, Alexander."

"Hi," I squeak. I shuffle the papers back into their folder, as if he can see what I'm looking at.

"It sounds like you're busy," he continues. "Should I try you another time?"

"No!" I interject, probably too quickly. Then I remember what Maria said about playing hard to get. "Well, I'm busy, but I can talk for a few minutes." I roll my eyes at myself.

"Great, because this will only take a few minutes."

Oh, here it comes, the line about how I'm a great girl, but he's met and fallen in love with Taylor Swift. I take a deep breath and brace myself.

"I was hoping you would join me for dinner next Wednesday night." I can hear his breathing, slightly too quick, through the silence. He actually sounds a little nervous. "You know, if you don't have plans."

"Ummm, let me check my calendar." I shuffle more papers so it sounds like I really am checking my calendar, although I know I have no plans. And even if I did, I'd cancel them. "Looks like I'm free. Yeah, I'd be happy to join you."

"Great, do you like Thai food? I know this awesome little Thai place we could go."

"Yeah, that sounds good." I try to keep my voice from squealing in the way Preston says it does when I get excited. I give Alexander my address, and he says he'll be there at seven.

When I hang up the phone, I have to hold onto the desk to keep myself from dancing around the room. Instead I do a little kicking jig under the table and sway in my seat. Then I pick up the phone to call Maria and give her the news.

CHAPTER 12

EVA KNOCKS ON MY DOOR at precisely eight a.m. on Thursday morning. I am downing a cappuccino (my newfound love) and trying to get my brain working after staying up half the night, pairing my new outfits with shoes and trying to figure out what I am going to wear. I pull out the mirror from my desk drawer and double check my hair. I tuck back the few strands that have come free from the loose bun I threw my hair into after the world's quickest shower this morning. Maybe next time I'll hit the snooze button a few less times and make sure I have time to wash my hair.

I open the door, and there stands a tiny woman, not more than five feet tall. Her red hair is pinned perfectly into a low ponytail and her makeup is flawless. I'm really wishing I had put more thought into my outfit, that I hadn't thrown on the basic dark jeans, white blouse, and casual blazer. I prefer to look put together and professional, especially for a first meeting with a client.

"Hi!" she chirps in a voice that sounds as though it's already been up for five hours. "I'm Eva. It's so nice to meet you. I can't wait to hear what you have planned for me." She grabs my hand and starts enthusiastically pumping it.

I introduce myself, offer her a bottle of water, and point her toward the purple armchair. She is so full of energy that as she speaks she seems to start floating, like a helium balloon. Each time she adjusts her sitting position, as if she's trying to reanchor herself. She is going on and on about how much she loves Nicholas Watson, how she's tried to meet him but it's never worked out, how she thinks we are going to get along so well. When I get the chance, I kindly interrupt her and get her to look over the legal paperwork. She barely glances at it when she signs her name, never actually looking at what she is signing. She is too busy talking and looking at me.

This should be an easy "accidental" meeting with fast turnaround time. Since I have set up meetings for clients with Nicholas before, I know what to expect on his part. Nicholas Watson is known for being very nice to all his fans. He never turns down an autograph (even in church at his grandmother's funeral, or so the story goes), and he stays to chat with fans after all of his red-carpet premieres. It doesn't hurt that he is the eternal bachelor, leaving open all sorts of possibilities in my clients' minds. It occurs to me to ask Eva how she had tried to meet Nicholas, but I haven't been able to get a word in edgewise; instead, I jot down my question on a post-it and put it in her file to ask later.

It's really just a matter of finding a meeting place that is comfortable for Eva. As spunky as she is, this shouldn't be a problem. Her lack of celebrity etiquette is clearly what has kept her from meeting him.

When I list the different services I offer—a meeting; a makeover and a meeting; a meeting with potential follow-up meetings—she insists that all she wants is a meeting.

"Oh, I don't need a makeover," she explains. And she's right. She is rather attractive and eye-catching. "I just need you to set up the meeting. I can take it from there."

"Well, I don't just set up meetings." She clearly wasn't listening to me during our previous phone calls. "I create the opportunity for you to meet in a comfortable setting. I provide coaching on what to say and how to act. It's a package deal."

"Can't you just tell me where he's going to be and when he's going to be there, and I'll show up? Can't we do it that way?"

"I find meetings are more successful when I accompany my client. That way, I can help ensure the meeting goes more or less as planned." I am still smiling but inside alarms are going off. I calm myself by remembering she's never done this before. Once she gets how it works, she'll be fine.

"Oh." She seems to think about this. "So I don't get a say in any of it?"

"Well, we come up with a plan together. And we make sure that you are comfortable with everything you need to do."

She looks a little worried. I am getting worried again too.

"It'll be fine," I reassure her. "I've arranged over two hundred meetings. You came to me for a reason, remember?"

This seems to calm her, more or less. She gives me a long, hard look. "Okay," she concedes. "We'll do it your way." Then she flashes me a huge smile, but I'm not so sure how sincere it is.

We go over all the information she has, and I am surprised to find how accurate it is. While she may not have been listening to what she was signing up for, she certainly did do her homework. On her own, she found most of what I have on file for Nicholas and some other interesting information that will be helpful, like he takes a meditation class every Tuesday afternoon. I've always known that he religiously studies meditation at the Calm Mind Institute of Santa Monica, but I didn't know which class he attended. A chatty, and newly hired, institute receptionist let it slip one day when I was calling to get information on classes for myself. As soon as she realized what she had done, she hung up the phone so fast that I wasn't able to get the information I was originally looking for.

I ask Eva where she got her information and, although she won't give me a straight answer, she assures me wholeheartedly that it is definitely accurate. For whatever reason, and against my better judgment, I don't press the issue.

I wonder for a brief moment if there are fans who know this much about Alexander. The thought of others having such intimate details of his personal life leaves me with the sour feeling of jealousy. Whether the jealousy comes from the possibility that fans may know more about him than I do or that someone could be gathering details to meet him, I'm not sure. The feeling I get from both scenarios is uncomfortable, so I focus my attention back to the task at hand: getting Eva to comply with my policies.

I present my plan to Eva, and she gets very excited. I can see her eyes light up when she imagines she'll be meditating right next to Nicholas Watson. Or, rather, pretending to meditate. She starts nodding her head a little and then looks up to the corner of the room as if lost in thought. After a short while I bring her back. "Eva?" I say, then louder, "EVA?"

She snaps to attention. "Oh, I'm sorry, I was just picturing it. Me, sitting there right next to Nicholas, both of us 'ommming' in unison." She relaxes her hands on the armrests, palms up, and her gaze strays back up to the ceiling, a calm smile spreading across her lips.

"Good! So you like the plan."

She continues staring out into space. While she is lost in thought, I make a quick phone call to enroll myself in the Tuesday afternoon class as a visiting meditator. I jot down the phone number for her to enroll as well as. I wave the paper in front of her, bringing her out of the trance.

"Your homework is to go to this website and read about meditation." I point to the address on the paper. "I need you back here on Monday for about an hour, and then we'll go to the class on Tuesday. I've also written down what you should wear for the class. It's really important that we look like we belong there and not like we're there for Nicholas. Got it?"

She takes the paper and nods at me. This time she actually reads it. "I can't wait! This is going to be perfect!" Then she reaches into her purse and pulls out a check, already written out, and slides it across the desk to me, the whole time giving me the same big not-so-sure-it's-sincere smile. She hops to her feet and bounces out the door.

CHAPTER
13

ON MONDAY MORNING AT eight a.m. on the dot, as I expected, there is that enthusiastic knock on my door. I open it to Eva's bright smile. She lunges forward and gives me a big hug. Trying to regain my composure I halfheartedly hug her back. We both take our seats, and Eva smiles at me, waiting.

"Did you do your homework?" I ask.

She looks for a moment, her smile fades just the slightest bit, and then she rebounds. "Of course. Meditating is the art of—" And she goes on with a long explanation of exactly what meditating is.

I sit staring, waiting for her to finish. She sure is thorough. When she's done, we go over the plan for tomorrow. She listens attentively as I tell her that I will get there first and find a mat near Nicholas', leaving just enough room for someone to squeeze in between us, which is exactly what she will do when she arrives. Then we will go through the meditation class and, at the end when we are given the opportunity to discuss our experience with our new neighbors, I will turn to Nicholas' nearest neighbor so he will have no choice but to turn to Eva. We role-play a few possible conversations on the class's topic (I was able to convince the nice woman who answered the phone to tell me which reading we'd be discussing under the guise that I want to get the most out of my new experience).

Eva had wonderful thoughts to share and insights on the topic. Since she had clearly done her homework, I skipped over the proper etiquette of meditating. As we hug goodbye I am beginning to think tomorrow's meeting has the potential to turn into one of my best yet, and so I completely dismiss my gut when it tells me I am forgetting something.

Before I head out on my weekly run to the newsstand, a quick chat with Frank the doorman and a few other sources around town, I gather all the old and picked-through tabloids and magazines. Something stops me in my tracks. There on the cover of *Celebrity Today* is the headline "Sexiest Men in the World." Right under that are pictures of four delicious-looking men, one of them being none other than Alexander Young. It would be so easy to get lost reading all about him, learning every detail I could possibly want to know, with so much information right at my fingertips. And that could just be the beginning. I could Google him. I could spend hours reading about him and every move he's ever made in public.

But then I close my eyes and picture that sweet grin he gave me in the parking lot. I remember how he smelled like strawberry gelato, and how he told me all about his travels, how I know so little about him and, perhaps, that is why this is working. I don't *need* to pretend to know nothing like my clients do, since I actually *do* know nothing. And I want to learn about him in the normal way. From him.

I open my eyes, smiling, toss the pile into the trash, and head out.

I arrive at the meditation class fifteen minutes early on Tuesday. I am excited about the meeting, not only because I think it will go well but also because I have always wanted to learn to meditate. Nicholas regularly gets to class early (the newly hired receptionist I had spoken to also let this slip), so I grab a blanket and walk into class to find my seat.

Nicholas Watson is there, already on his mat in the full lotus. Although I've been arranging these meetings for years, I still find it surprising that a rock star, known for riotous crowd-surfing, practices meditation. I sit my mat down just far enough away for someone to squeeze between us. Quietly, I maneuver into a crossed-leg position and try to pretend to clear my mind.

At exactly seven minutes before class starts, Eva walks in, just as we had planned. Only she's not walking in, she's *parading* in. I don't think it's the norm for anyone to come to meditation class decked out in bright pink gym clothes, full makeup, curled hair, and platform shoes. *Spiked* platform shoes. Not to mention the bright purple and green meditation mat.

I sit and stare straight ahead, breathing deeply, trying to order the thoughts that are filling my mind that's now racing fast. What is she thinking? This is not in our plan! She finds me and Nicholas and clumsily scoots her way into the spot between us, mumbling, "Excuse me," and "Pardon me," in a whisper-shout. Then she looks at me and winks.

She. Winks. At. Me.

She has broken my number one rule. Never, no matter what happens, ever, acknowledge that you know me.

Eva leans over to Nicholas and whispers, "Cool pose."

Nicholas turns to Eva with a polite, though unencouraging, smile. Then as his eyes meet Eva's, they grow very, very wide. It looks as though he's hiding some emotion, like a master trying to train a dog that has just urinated on the floor. Through gritted teeth, he hisses at her, "I'm meditating!"

Uh-oh. Where is the loving celebrity who chatted with a child for forty-five minutes while waiting for her mom? The one who always smiles and is notorious for being overkind? I am definitely missing something here. Has my focus on Alexander put me this far off my game?

Eva smiles back, ever so clueless and says, "Oh, yes, so am I." Then she scoots closer to him.

It hits me, like a slap in the face, that Eva never had any intentions of going along with my plan. All she wanted was an in—a way to get close enough to Nicholas so she could do it her way.

Nicholas looks back at her with an expression I've only seen on him while singing hard, anger-filled songs. "How did you know I was here? I told you to never talk to me again!" Before Eva has the chance to respond, he stands up, grabs his mat and leaves, stopping only at the front desk to say something to the receptionist. The receptionist looks at Eva, then into her book, and makes a note.

Eva turns to me, and I give her the most disapproving look I can muster without bursting into a twenty-minute lecture on how stupid her actions are. Basically, I give her the facial equivalent of the middle finger. *You are not taking ME down on this sinking ship!*

A man in a soothing voice walks into the room and starts to talk us through relaxing our bodies. I hear a slight sobbing next to me and ignore it. The man starts talking about how to bring kindness into our lives. The sobbing gets louder. He glances toward Eva and then continues. She continues sobbing. I am trying harder than ever to completely ignore Eva, to pretend as though I am enjoying everything the man is saying, when really all I want is to grab my things and run out of the room. But I'm stuck. I know if I leave, people will know I'm with Eva, and that's not something I can afford to let out. Especially now.

After what feels like an hour of her sobbing, but in reality was probably only five minutes or so, the receptionist comes in and quietly leads Eva out of the room and out of the building.

I turn my full attention to the man who is still speaking because, right now, I need to hear all I can about kindness.

After class is over, I decide to go straight home. I am not in the mood for work, and I know I won't be able to get anything done. I feel totally, completely betrayed and defeated. As I walk into my apartment, my cell phone buzzes, and I remember that I had turned it on vibrate to not disturb the class. There are ten messages. Before I can dial my voicemail, it starts vibrating again. I see that it's Eva calling.

"What?" I snap into the phone. So much for kindness.

"How could you," Eva begins.

"How could *I*? I didn't do anything! All I did was sit there on a mat and watch your train wreck! Clearly you HAVE met Nicholas before, and you kept that information from me. And clearly he remembers you for whatever psychotic thing you did to him! What did you do?" I close my eyes, take a deep breath, and drop onto my sofa. Then, in a calmer voice, I begin, "Know what? I don't want to know what you did. I don't want to hear any of it. You came to me for my help and hid information from me. We spent time coming up with a plan that you never intended to use. That time could've been spent on a client who really needs my help."

"But I did need your help; I still do," she sobs into the phone.

"No, you could have ruined my career in there. My entire business could have been ruined because you wanted to stalk Nicholas Watson. Please, just stay away from Nicholas, and stay away from me."

"But we have a contract," she interrupts. The old Eva is back, the sobbing one has vanished. "You didn't deliver. In fact, you just sat there and gave me dirty looks. You should have jumped in and helped me. Isn't that what I paid you for?"

I start pacing around the coffee table. "No. You paid me to arrange a meeting, under my terms, with Nicholas Watson. You were supposed to follow our plan and you didn't. I can't do anything without my client's cooperation."

"So you're not going to help me?"

I can't believe her. "No."

"Well," she breathes, too calmly, "I'm sorry to hear that." And she hangs up.

Kindness. Happiness. Be kind to others. The meditation leader's words hum in my ears. I toss my phone onto the sofa, kick off my shoes, grab a tub of rocky road ice cream, and plop myself down in front of the TV. I switch the channel to Lifetime.

That is where I sit until midnight, when I shuffle into bed.

CHAPTER
14

THE SUN PEEKS INTO MY bedroom as I wake and glance at the clock. Seven a.m. I sit up and see the empty ice cream container on my nightstand. I let out a big sigh, throw it away, and remind myself that today is a new day. A new day in which I have a date with Alexander. To get ready for the day, I smile to myself and shove yesterday to the back of my mind where I don't have to think about it.

I get to the office and make myself a coffee. I will spend the morning doing research since I don't have any clients scheduled. A new round of tabloids are waiting for me, though I find myself staring at the wall, thinking about my date with Alexander tonight. This is officially a date. We are going to dinner. He is picking me up.

I flip open my computer and search for Thai restaurants in the area that celebrities like to frequent. Two come up. I start reading about them, and then I get to the paragraph about Nicholas Watson and how he eats at one of them every week. I shudder and decide that I'll let wherever Alexander takes me be a surprise. I'm reaching for the tabloids, when there's a knock on the door. I feverishly click on my phone calendar to see if I have an appointment I forgot about. Nothing.

The knock comes again, more serious sounding this time. I jump out of my seat and hurry to the door. When I open it, I see a nice-looking man in a suit, with a charming smile.

"Olivia Fowler?"

"That's me," I say, using my most professional voice.

He pulls out an envelope from his jacket pocket and hands it to me. "Here you go."

While I open the envelope, he leaves, walking quickly down the hall.

I pull out the letter and read-walk to my desk, hearing the door click shut behind me. I can't believe what I'm reading.

Eva is suing me.

I flop onto my chair and toss the paper onto my desk. Just then the phone rings. Caller ID reads Unknown.

"I want my money back," Eva spurts into the phone before I have the chance to say hello.

"I can see that," I say in a monotone, trying not to sound too angry or defeated. "Thing is, you signed a contract. I provided my service as outlined in the contract. Any judge will see that."

"Any judge will see that you sat in the meditation class and ignored me. You didn't provide any help."

When I first started my business, I paid a small fortune to a lawyer to come up with a law-suit–proof contract. We went over it a thousand times to make sure that there was no way I could be held liable for my client's or the celebrity's actions. I know that if this goes to court, Eva doesn't stand a chance.

"There's a stalker clause and you fraudulently represented yourself. I'm not giving you your money back."

"Of course you are," she replies calmly. Too calmly. "You know I can meet Nicholas again."

I walk over to my desk, move the tabloids to the side, and sit.

"I told you, I'm not going to help you meet him again. I'm done working with you."

"Not like that. I'm going to meet him on my own, like before. And I'm going to tell him all about your little business. Not to mention, no doubt the local news would love to hear about this predicament of ours."

I don't know how to respond. So I don't. If I open my mouth to speak, I'm afraid all that will come out is a loud sob.

"Unless, of course, you give me my money back," she continues. "In which case you will receive a contract from me stating that I will never speak of our meeting to anyone again. Ever."

I am still silent.

"Think about it," she hisses. Then she hangs up.

I am completely taken aback. I try to hold in my tears. I can't return Eva's money. I've never given money back, and I don't ever intend to. My clients sign that contract for a reason...and it clearly states no money back under any circumstances. Then again, I've never had a client threaten to tell a celebrity about my business or even have a reason to request their money back.

What if she does tell Nicholas? Would he believe her? Because really, from what I saw, Nicholas seems to think or, rather, know that Eva is crazy. So why would he listen to her?

But what if he does? I've worked so hard to build my business. This business is my life. And if Nicholas finds out about it, surely he would tell his friends.

And if the press knows, this could eventually get back to Alexander. This is definitely not the way I want *him* to find out.

Maria would know what to do. Only it's Wednesday morning and Maria has her weekly company meeting on Wednesday. I lay my head down on the desk and hope an answer will magically come to me. Just then my phone starts ringing. I check the caller ID. Unknown again. Seriously? Does Eva really think I want to talk to her?

"What?" I spit into the phone.

There's a pause.

I clear my throat, as it occurs to me that it may not be Eva. I try to say in a sweeter voice, "Hello?"

"Hi," a sexy voice replies. "It's Alexander. Ummm…do you want to call me back later?"

At the sound of his voice my body relaxes. I rest my forehead in my hand. "Oh! I'm so sorry! I was just on the phone with—" Crap! I can't tell Alexander about this! "I just thought it was someone else."

"Is everything okay?"

Yes, I want to say. I want to say, *Tonight I get to go out with you, and I will forget all about this horrible problem.* "It's just work stuff. It'll all be fine," I lie.

"Okay, good." He pauses. "Do you want to talk about it?"

Ha! Do I want to talk about it? I'd love to talk about it with Alexander. He'd probably have great perspective on the topic. But no way am I going to chance ruining what we have going. "It's all right. Let's just talk about something other than work. Like tonight."

"About tonight." He pauses again. "I'm going to need to reschedule."

This is not my day.

"Hello?" he asks.

"Yeah, I'm here."

"My publicist just called, and I have this thing she really wants me to go to. She says it will be good for my career." He lets out a sigh. "Is it okay if we make it another night?"

Again I gulp back a tear and muster all the energy I have to make it sound like I'm not even phased by this. "Of course!" I respond, probably too cheerily. "I've got this work thing I need to figure out anyway. Let's just do it another night."

"Great! How about Friday night? I mean, if you don't have any other plans."

"Friday sounds good," I reply, feeling better but still fighting the urge to cry.

As soon as we hang up, I yank open my bottom drawer, pull out a package of red licorice, and start munching in hopes the tight knot forming in my stomach will relax. If this week doesn't start to look up, I may not fit into my new outfits by the time Friday night rolls around.

Once I finish half the package of licorice I convince myself to put the rest of it far away, like in the back of a cupboard behind a large box. I fish through my purse for my mirror. A piece of paper falls out, and I pick it up to put it back in my purse. It's Charlie's business card.

Charlie would know what to do! He's a publicist, he deals with personal tragedies like this day in and day out. Plus, maybe he knows how Nicholas Watson would react if he found out about me. I grab my phone and dial.

"Hey, Olivia," he answers.

"Hi, Charlie." I ask all the polite questions before I delve into my problem.

"I seem to have a bit of a problem, and I was hoping to get your perspective on it." I wait for his response.

"Of course," he says. "Does it have to do with Alexander Young?"

"No." I stop myself before I divulge anything about Alexander, remembering that whatever I tell Charlie, Preston will hear. "It's a client problem."

I tell Charlie about my first meeting with Eva, and the meditation class, and how Nicholas freaked when he saw her. When I finish talking, all I hear is the click-click of his pen.

He lets out a big breath. "I think you've gotta give her the money back."

"Really? You don't think I stand a chance?" I ask, surprised by his quick answer. His chair squeaks, and then I hear a door shut.

"You'd win in court. But I'm worried about how Nicholas Watson would react to this." I can hear his voice changing from Charlie-the-friend to Charlie-the-publicist. "He may be a nice guy, but remember when he sued that tabloid for defamation of character when it printed that article that claimed he was sleeping with Collin Farrell's girlfriend? And he won? He also sued that company for using a frog that looked like him in their commercials, saying they were making money off of his likeness. He won that one too. I don't think he'd be pleased to find out someone was making money by selling meetings with him that he didn't even know about. I'm sorry I don't have a different answer for you, Olivia, but I think you'll be committing career suicide if you don't play Eva's game."

I lean my forehead onto my hand and close my eyes.

"You think it's that bad, huh?" I ask, just to make sure.

"I think it's worse," he says. After a few seconds of silence he asks, in the Charlie-the-friend voice, "Do you need to borrow some money? I won't tell Preston."

"Thanks, Charlie," I say, completely defeated. "But no, I have the money; it's the principle. Giving the money back is like saying I was wrong. And you know me, I hate being wrong."

Once we hang up, I pull out Eva's file, and that's when I see it: the big post-it note to remind me to ask Eva how she tried to meet Nicholas. There it is, proof. Proof that this is my fault, that I was wrong. I wasn't as thorough as I normally am...as I should have been. Had I asked her that simple question, I would've known better than to take her on as a client. But I was so distracted that Alexander had asked me on another date that I ignored my gut feeling. I totally overlooked the obvious.

Now I know Charlie is right. I have to give Eva her money back.

CHAPTER 15

THAT NIGHT, BY SEVEN O'CLOCK, I'm sitting on my sofa, already in my favorite frumpy flannel pajamas, my hair in a loose messy bun perched on the top of my head. I'm about to start watching *The Princess Bride*. A tub of rocky road ice cream is on the table in front of me, unopened—the only thing I could find the energy to get for dinner. The doorbell rings and, for just a second, I think that maybe it's Alexander, that maybe I completely misunderstood our conversation and he hadn't actually cancelled. Remembering I'm in my pajamas at an absurdly early time of day, I consider not answering the door, just in case.

Thunk. Thunk. I can hear someone shuffling around outside. Slowly and stealthlike, I sneak to the door, avoiding all windows, trying to get a better view of who it might be. Maria is still in her meeting; no one else I know stops by unannounced.

"I'm so stupid," I hear a familiar voice whisper outside. *Charlie*?

I step back from the door and look through the peephole. It is Charlie. Why is he here? Without thinking, I swing open the door.

"Hey," I say.

At first he just looks at me from head to toe, as if confused. He looks at his watch, then back at me, and, poorly, tries to hide a grin. "Am I interrupting something?"

"What, you've never had a bad day?" I step back and let him in. He is carrying a big white bag with grease seeping through it.

"I thought you might need some cheering up." He walks over to the table and puts down the bag. "Have you eaten yet?"

I start giggling. "I was just about to." I pick up the tub of ice cream and flop onto the sofa. "You're welcome to join me. Spoons are in the drawer under the microwave."

"Ice cream? And *The Princess Bride*? You're lucky I came over." He walks over and takes the tub out of my hands before I can open it. "I had something a little better in mind." He pulls two things out of the bag, both wrapped in yellow paper with bright red stickers on them. "You still like these, don't you?" he asks, and starts the movie without waiting for an answer.

Melted cheese, chili, and pickles waft out of the deli paper he is handing me. I don't even need to unwrap it to know what it is. "A Tommy's burger?" I start to strip off, one greasy layer at a time, all that is keeping me from pure heaven. "This is way better than ice cream."

"I'm glad you still like them." He watches me devour my burger as a glob of warm chili drips down my chin, and then he smiles and starts on his.

When we were in high school and Preston just got his driver's license, Maria and I would beg him and Charlie to take us with them wherever they were going. Of course no teenage guy wants his little sister hanging around, cramping his style. So my mom would convince him and Charlie to take us to the mall, where they could keep an eye on us without actually having to hang out with us.

And every once in a while, if they were in a really good mood, Preston and Charlie would take us to Tommy's. We thought we were so cool, eating dinner with older guys, even if one of them was my brother. All these years later, the burgers still taste delicious and remind me of more carefree days.

We eat our burgers and watch the movie, Charlie reciting his favorite lines along with the actors, and me mock-dying during each death scene. Soon we are laughing, relaxing, having a good time, just like when we were in high school. In fact, I don't think about Eva and her money and even forget how excited I was about my date with Alexander and how disappointed I am that he rescheduled. When the movie is over and we're both stuffed with burgers and fries and chili, I get up and stretch. I'm so exhausted, I can't wait to get to bed.

Charlie looks at me and sits up straight.

"Thanks for coming over, Charlie. This was fun." I yawn.

"Yeah." He starts to stand. "We should do it again sometime; you know, without all the...bad stuff."

Just as I was about to agree, my cell phone starts buzzing. It's nine p.m. Maria! I grab the phone and start jabbering to Maria about my day, forgetting about Charlie. I start throwing trash away and turning off the TV and lights.

"I guess I'd better be going," Charlie whispers to me.

I tell Maria to hold on and flip the phone onto my shoulder. "Okay. Thanks for dinner." I give him a one-armed hug.

"Anytime." He smiles, pauses. When neither of us say anything, he puts up his hand, says bye and leaves.

"Was that Charlie?" Maria asks through the phone.

"What? Oh, yeah. He just brought over some dinner." Then I tell Maria about my day and listen to her complain about how boring her Wednesday meeting was, before I cuddle up in my bed and finally go to sleep.

CHAPTER
16

I T'S OUR SECOND DATE, AND I'm even more
nervous than I was before our first, if that's possible.
Alexander insisted on picking me up at home and how
could I turn him down? I can't exactly say, "I'm sorry. I'm
hiding a huge secret from you that will probably make you
stop speaking to me and wish we'd never met." So instead,
I was up until midnight, cleaning every nook and cranny
just in case he insists on coming in. And I made sure I took
all my tabloids to the office yesterday so he won't see them.
Not to mention any files I had brought home in the past
few days.

I feel a lump welling up deep inside me. At knowing
that I'm lying to Alexander. *You're not lying,* I try to reason

with myself. *This has nothing to do with him. You can tell him when you're ready...once you know him better.* I've had this conversation with myself numerous times over the past couple of weeks. And although I seem to agree with myself on how I'm handling this, I still feel that lump every time I think about it. And it seems to grow bigger every time I talk to him.

Once again I swallow it down and try to distract myself. This time I check my lipstick in the mirror. Content with my lips, I look down at my outfit...one I bought on my shopping spree last week. Tonight I'm wearing a casual blue wrap dress that, according to Maria, makes me look voluptuous. I hope Alexander thinks so.

The doorbell rings, and I let out a deep breath, smile at myself in the mirror, and then grab a book to carry to the door so that Alexander doesn't suspect I've been trying to make myself look perfect for the last three hours. I can see through the living-room window that he is looking out over the piazza, his hand casually tucked in the pocket of his dark jeans. He looks perfect—a slight breeze ruffling the curls at his neck, those sexy arms hiding behind the button-up shirt. I am standing there, staring at him, when I realize I need to answer the door. I run a hand down my dress to smooth it out and step forward.

As I open the door he turns to me. "I was starting to think you weren't home," he teases. There's that vein on his temple. "These are for you." He holds out a small bouquet of miniature calla lilies.

I reach for the flowers and notice I'm still holding the paperback. I set the book on the table by the door and take the flowers. "Thank you, they're beautiful." I smile at him. "Would you like to come in while I put these in water?" He hesitates and then walks in and sits on the green armchair as I turn to go to the kitchen. *Ugh! I should've hugged him!*

"This is a nice place you've got," he says. "That's quite the view, with the tropical garden and all. It reminds me of this island in the South Pacific I visited once."

"Thanks. I find it relaxing. After a hard day at work, I like to sit out there and stare at the plants." I reach for a vase from under the sink and run water into it. "I like to close my eyes and breathe in the air, pretend I'm somewhere tropical." I place the flowers on the coffee table.

"Should we go?" He stands up and puts his hand out for mine. His eyebrows are raised and he has on that sweet boyish grin.

I put my hand in his, and we walk out the door.

When we get to the sidewalk he pauses. "Is something wrong?" I ask.

"Well, do you mind if I drive us this time? I mean, if you want to take your own car that's fine, I just—"

I can't keep the smile from creeping across my face. "Yes, of course you can drive." A little giggle escapes. "I don't mind if you drive at all."

When we reach his car, he opens my door for me and I get in, careful to tuck my skirt beneath so as not to flash him. He turns on the ignition, and music blasts through the speakers. He mumbles a quick apology as he lowers the volume, and it takes me a moment to realize that it's jazz music he's listening to. Our conversation flows naturally as he navigates through the crowded streets, and then to less traveled ones on the east side of town.

"So where are we going?"

"It's a surprise." He grins. "You'll figure it out." He pats me on the knee, sending my heart into a whirl.

Soon we zoom out of the residential neighborhood, and we wind up a road with several other cars. I see a lit-up building ahead of us. Below the city shines. Our conversation continues.

We pull into an empty parking spot that's a ways from a beautiful white building. It is large, lined with big windows. Bulging out the top of the building is a large dome. There are two smaller domes, one on each end. Then I realize where we are: I fondly remember this place from my childhood.

"Oh, wow!" I gasp. "I haven't been here in years!"

As I sit slack-jawed, staring at the building, he comes around and opens my door. I step out and continue to stare. "Every summer my parents would bring my brother and me here to look at the stars and the city lights. My mom would tell us about the constellations above, and my dad would tell us about the buildings and landmarks below."

Alexander turns and looks with me. "I was hoping you would enjoy this. The Griffith Park Observatory has some pretty breathtaking views of the city and the stars. Where I grew up there weren't any observatories, but we'd camp in the backyard—my brother, my mom, and I. Mom would make up all these crazy stories about the stars and how they got there."

He shuts the car door and pulls a backpack out of the trunk. As he slings the bag over his shoulder, he wraps an arm around me and guides me toward the expansive front lawn with the tall statue in the middle. "Of course when we got older, my dad told us the truth. My mom says she's glad she wasn't there when Dad told us that stars aren't really marshmallows toasted by the sun."

When we get to the entrance, Alexander pulls open the door and waits for me to walk through it. We spend an hour wandering the building, from room to room, hall to hall. He keeps his arm gently around me the whole time. We talk about everything—places we've visited and would like to, childhood memories, even history. We have so much in common that I completely forget he is a celebrity...until we get cornered by some southern tourists who can't believe they finally found a "ceelebertee" on their last night in town. And they are just thrilled to pieces that Aunt Mable is "gonner flip when she sees this here picture." Alexander is cordial and friendly to them, which, of course, I take due note of. The friendlier he is to fans, the more likely he will be open to my line of work...when I tell him what it is I really do. Whenever that may be.

In fact, Alexander is so friendly that we talk with these fans for at least twenty minutes and he takes no less than ten photos with them. He is so attentive to their questions about his next movie that I begin to wonder if he remembers that he's on a date with me, until he glances at me with those gorgeous eyes and gives me his crooked grin as a way of apologizing, a sort of secret between the two of us. It feels as though we are moving together as a couple, developing a mutual understanding. Until...

I notice that while we are talking with these fans, he doesn't have his arm around me. And he doesn't put it back around me until they are gone and out of sight.

Once the fans are gone, he pulls me into him, wrapping his arms tightly around my waist. "Sorry about that," he whispers. "I think it's important to be friendly to the people that keep you working." Then he smiles and points out a display across the room, and pulls me with him toward it.

I obediently follow.

Once we've made our way through the building, we go out to the observation platform where we can see the entire city.

"Let's see if we can find where you live." He squints his eyes and looks out to the west.

"Hmmm…I think it's somewhere over there," I say as I point to a group of tall buildings.

"That's right. We drove by that building with the yellow sign on the top floor," he says. I can't believe I am here with Alexander, and he is not only thinking about where I live but seems to be using his semipermanent memory to remember it.

"Can you see your place?" I ask, hoping he doesn't think I'm intruding. He is a celebrity after all, and I'm just an average girl.

"I live right around there," he says as he points to several small clusters of lights surrounding pockets of black. Then he turns to me with a peaceful smile, his arm resting on the railing. "I'll have to have you over sometime."

Me? Going to Alexander's house? I'm ready. Let's skip this whole date thing and go. The couple next to us, discussing something in loud voices, most likely in Italian, brings me back to reality. Then I remember this is only our second date. I suppose going to his place wouldn't be very appropriate.

He takes my hand and leads me to a staircase. When we reach the top, he walks us over to a well-lit area and puts down a blanket that he's pulled out of his bag.

"What's this?" I ask.

"This," he says, as he helps me to the ground, "is dinner." He takes several containers of Thai food out of his bag and puts them on the blanket in front of us. Then he pulls out a small bottle of wine and two wine glasses. "I wanted us to be able to really sit and talk without the interruptions of waiters and…other people."

I melt at the thought that he doesn't want to share me with anyone. I want to pinch myself to make sure this is all really happening. I thought our first date was perfect, but, so far, tonight seems even better.

"Since you like Thai food, I decided to pick some up for us." He puts a small, ceramic plate in front of me. "I'm really sorry I couldn't make it Wednesday. It was a publicity thing that came up last minute. That doesn't happen often, but when it does, I can't really get out of it. Maybe someday you can join me." He pours me some white wine.

I give him a simple smile, trying to hide the excitement that is spilling over as it registers that he just referred to our future, for the second time. He pours himself a glass and scoots across the blanket so he is sitting right next to me.

Just then, an official-looking man in a beige suit comes toward us. I prepare emotionally for Alexander to move away from me, but as he leans toward the man, he places his hand on my knee. The man whispers into his ear, and Alexander nods, smiles and quietly says thank you to him. Then he focuses his attention back to me.

"Thank you for joining me this evening, Olivia." He holds up his glass. "To a wonderful star-filled night." We clink glasses, and before I can bring the glass to my lips, he leans in and kisses my cheek.

He takes a sip of his wine, and I feel heat rise to my face. To hide it, I take a big sip of wine. He dishes some food onto my plate, then his own, and we start eating. He asks me about my family and my work, and I manage to almost entirely avoid the work topic by talking about Preston and how we weren't really as close when we were young but now are like best friends. He tells me about how his dad left when he was a teenager and his brother became his father figure, even though he is only four years older.

We are so involved in our conversation that it doesn't strike me as odd that we haven't seen anyone around for hours. It is just Alexander and me alone with the stars. So when he wraps his arm around my shoulder and pulls me in close, I still have my fan guard up. He, though, is completely at ease. Here I am, staring into those seductive green eyes just a few inches away from me. The only sound around is a soft breeze rustling the trees below us as he reaches up and brushes a few hairs behind my ear.

I can barely breathe. But right now, I am not telling myself not to be nervous because he is a regular person just like me. Because it doesn't occur to me that he's not. He is just a handsome man I am on a date with. I embrace the pounding of my heart and the fluttering in my stomach as he leans in and kisses me.

He takes his time as we embrace and kiss. He knows just how to kiss me, just where to place his hand at the back of my neck. The sweetness of his lips, the eager patience of his hands. I am certainly gone. There is no turning back now. I may as well put my heart on a plate with the food and hand it over to Alexander.

I hear the faint buzzing of my cell phone in my purse, and he gives the same half-grin as when we first went to coffee. *There's that sexy vein again.* "I guess we should probably get going."

I want to yell, "No, let's not! Let's stay here forever!" But instead I nod and start to gather our things. I look around us and find that there isn't a single person nearby. *I wonder if it's later than I think.*

As we reach the bottom of the stairs I see why. A handful of men in suits, upscale security guards, stand with their hands folded in front of them, subtly scanning the people who are gazing at the stars. Behind them, a series of ropes hang, cordoning off the stairs to an area. Our area.

Alexander is walking next to me but at a slight distance. The man in the beige suit appears again. Alexander walks up to him and shakes his hand. They exchange a few words, and then he jogs to catch up to me, smiling.

I pretend not to notice as the ropes are taken down and the public is allowed back into the area where we were just picnicking. I know that I should be analyzing what just happened—research for my clients—but I don't. Instead I smile back at Alexander, and when he puts his hand on my knee as he slides into the car, all I can think about is when I will see him again.

CHAPTER 17

WHEN I MEET MARIA for brunch the next morning she doesn't even have to ask how my night went. She can tell by the smile pasted on my face.

"That good, eh?"

"No." I take a sip of my cappuccino. "Even better." I give her a breezy account of the evening, not wanting to share all of it with anyone, afraid it might make it less real.

"It was that great? Not one thing for me to analyze?" she complains.

"Well," I hesitate, hoping that I'm making something out of nothing. "There was one thing."

Maria sits up straight and squints her eyes like she does when she wants her coworkers to know how smart she is. Her silence is a sign for me to continue.

"It was just a little weird that whenever a fan came around, he wouldn't—" As it comes out of my mouth it sounds so minor. "He would take his arm from me. As if he didn't want anyone to know he was *with* me."

She chews on the end of her straw. "Hmmm." She looks to the ceiling, thinking. "Are you sure? Maybe you were being hypersensitive because his fans are your potential clients."

Up until now that thought hadn't occurred to me, that one of those people at the observatory could walk into my office tomorrow to hire me to make her dream come true. And then as she opens the office door, BAM! It's the lady who was hanging out with Alexander Young, not the professional who knows all the secrets of the celebrities but not the celebrities themselves. Then I think about how Alexander has no idea what I do, and I am drowning in overwhelming guilt. He went out of his way for us to have a normal date. One without interruptions. The kind of interruptions I create for my clients.

"You're right." I lie to Maria for the first time ever, not wanting to verbalize my guilt. "That's probably what it was."

CHAPTER 18

MARIA AND I CROSS THE street to the Brickyard Pub where we are meeting Preston and Charlie.

"You never told me why Charlie was at your place a few weeks ago," she starts.

I look at her, wondering what she is talking about.

"That night I called. I heard his voice in the background?" she persists.

"Oh!" It comes back to me. "I had a horrible day and needed some work advice. He just brought dinner over. I guess he was in the neighborhood."

Maria lifts an eyebrow at me.

"What?" I ask.

"He was in the neighborhood?" she asks. "He lives in Pasadena. That's twenty miles away. Not considering traffic. In Los Angeles, that's like stopping by the moon because you're near the sun."

I have no idea what she is getting at. She rolls her eyes at me.

We open the door to the bar and find Charlie and Preston already sitting at a table. They hug us both, and we order our drinks.

Almost immediately, Preston starts grilling me. "So, Liv, how's work going?"

"Great. I've got a couple of meetings set up for next week. I'm doing some research on a few big celebrities who I'm expecting to get requests for. Things are good."

"Oh, good. I'm glad you worked out that little mess," he adds.

I glance at Charlie. He must've said something to Preston about Eva. Charlie turns away. He promised not to say anything.

"Yeah," I mumble, "I got that straightened out."

"I am so glad," Preston continues. "I mean, you could've been in a really big mess there. I may not fully approve of your line of work, but that doesn't mean I want your business to go down the drain, and all because of one person."

I look at Charlie again. He nods along with Preston. I can't understand how he can be so guiltless after promising not to tell anyone about Eva.

Charlie catches my gaze. I am getting more and more furious by the second. He pulls the beer bottle away from his lips and stops agreeing with Preston. I decide to be confrontational.

"Yes, Preston," I begin, "you're right. A client tried to take advantage of a meeting gone bad. I gave her money back, and I've moved on. Do we really need to harp on it?"

Charlie looks confused. So does Preston.

"What?" Preston asks. "You gave a client her money back? What happened? Is everything okay?" He leans forward; his eyes soften.

Charlie is silent. Maria is silent. Preston is waiting for an explanation. They are all staring at me.

"Isn't that what you're talking about? Didn't—" I glance at Charlie, and he subtly shakes his head. I am so confused.

"I was talking about Alexander Young." Preston raises an eyebrow. "How relieved I am that you came to your senses and didn't go on a date with him."

Maria giggles, and I shoot her a dirty look. "What do you mean I didn't go on a date with Alexander?"

"Didn't you decide not to—" Preston asks, then looks at Charlie. "Charlie, you said Alexander is dating someone."

"Does anyone in this family ever connect the dots?" Maria says under her breath.

"I did hear he is dating someone," Charlie says to Preston. "I just assumed it was—" He lowers his head and lets out a sigh. Maria rolls her eyes.

"It's YOU he's dating?" Preston accuses. "YOU are the girl he's so into?"

"What do you mean?" I choke on my beer, trying to hide the overwhelming feeling of joy.

Charlie lets out another sigh. He grabs his beer bottle and motions to the waitress to get him another. "I heard from a colleague that he's been dating someone and trying really hard to keep it under wraps. To keep her protected. We all assumed it was because she was a big celebrity. Not—"

"Not what, Charlie?" I ask.

"Not just a normal average girl," he finishes.

Maria sucks in her breath loudly.

"Oh, I see," I respond. Even though it's just Charlie, being called "average" stings. I start wondering if that's how Alexander sees me, as average. Of course not. I push the thought away.

"Come on, Liv," Preston snaps, "you're no Taylor Swift."

Charlie elbows Preston and shoots him a dirty look.

I stand up. I don't want to hear any of it. "Well, turns out I'm good enough for Alexander." I turn and walk out the door with Maria following. As we are walking away, I hear Charlie grumble and swear at Preston. I keep moving.

Once we get out the door Maria catches up to me and puts her hand on my shoulder.

"Hey, what's going on? Are you okay?" she asks. "It's not like you to get upset over something Charlie or Preston says."

I stop and realize that I'm so worked up I have to catch my breath.

"I don't know. I just wish Preston would—" I'm not sure how to finish the sentence.

"Respect you and your career?" she asks.

"Yes. Why can't he see me as an adult?"

Maria points to a bench nearby, a little bit away from the crowd waiting to get into the Pub. We sit down and I wrap my jacket around me.

"And what's Charlie's problem? Why is he attacking me all of a sudden?" I ask.

"I don't think Charlie meant it as an insult. I think he just meant you're down-to-earth and not a celebrity. You know Charlie thinks the world of you."

I stop picking at my nails and look at Maria. "Charlie doesn't think the world of me. He thinks of me as Preston's little sister."

Maria rolls her eyes. "I know you don't see it, but he thinks pretty highly of you. You're not just a kid to him."

"But I am to Preston," I add.

Maria takes a breath. She reaches over and puts my hand between hers. "Remember when we first started hanging out?" she asks.

"Of course I do. We were in that awful science class together. There was no way I was going to dissect that frog. No one should put a seventh grader through that."

Maria laughs. "Right. You asked the teacher if you could dissect a rubber frog instead."

I let out a small chuckle. "Yeah. But what does this have to do with Preston?"

"Well, when we were walking home that day with Preston, you wouldn't stop talking about how cruel the teacher was. You went on forever."

I wait for her to get to the point. She leans toward me and raises her eyebrows, hoping I'll make some crazy connection.

"The next day," she continues, "when we got home from cheerleading practice, there was a rubber frog waiting for you in your room. Scalpel, plastic tray, and all."

I burst into laughter. "That's right! And the little sign that was next to him, No Frogs Were Harmed in the Making of This Rubber Toy."

"That's Preston. All he wants is to protect you and see you happy. Even then, before—"

"Before my parents died." I finally understand what Maria is trying to say. "And now he feels even more responsible for my safety and happiness."

"A big, famous celebrity can be pretty intimidating, you know. All we read about in the tabloids is how famous people cheat and get divorced and live miserable lives. We rarely hear the good stuff. Even though many of them are happy."

She has a point. It is rare to hear good things about celebrities and their relationships. That's probably why Alexander is keeping our relationship a secret.

"You're right. Preston has said so many times that his main job, especially now, is to keep me safe. And I suppose Alexander could look like a potential threat to someone who doesn't know him."

"Think about it, Liv. Even you didn't want anything to do with him at first. And that wasn't only because of your line of work."

"Which Preston also hates," I add.

"He doesn't hate it. He just doesn't see it as stable. I don't think he understands your real talent for it because he doesn't understand your clients."

"He's so practical. And that is something that my clients are definitely not."

Maria nods.

"I just wish he would be more supportive. Or at least try to understand. He's all I've got."

"You know, your parents would be so proud of you."

I giggle. "Yeah, my dad would probably want to come along on the meetings."

Maria giggles too.

"But that's not something Preston would do. He'll come around eventually. He may never understand what you do, but someday he may appreciate how you help your clients."

I lean over, put my arm around Maria, and rest my head against hers. "Thanks for listening and being here."

"Of course. That's what friends are for."

CHAPTER
19

ALEXANDER'S PICTURE POPS UP as my phone chimes. I feel a smile involuntarily spread across my face, and I instinctively close the file I'm looking at on my desk.

"Good morning, beautiful," he purrs into the phone.

"Hi there," I respond. "Early morning at work?"

"Yeah. Just finishing up, actually." He sounds a little nervous, which makes me nervous. "So—"

So? This can't be good. I brace myself. Is he breaking up with me? Wait, are we even at a point where breaking up is possible? *Olivia! Get a grip! You've got to stop freaking out every time he pauses!* I take a deep breath and before

I beat myself up too badly, I remember that this nervousness is what makes me good at my job, what pushes me to find situations in which my clients are comfortable meeting their idols. I take another deep breath.

"So?" I repeat back.

"So I have this thing." He pauses again. "I was hoping you would join me."

Yes! I want to yell. "A thing? Sure," I say coolly, "I'll join you for a thing."

"Great." He sounds a little relieved. Then he continues more cautiously. "But it's sort of a red carpet thing. You know, with fans and paparazzi and other people in my field."

"Oh." My heart is pounding. "Okay. That sounds fun."

"It's the premiere for that movie I filmed last year, *Solemn Nights.*"

"Sounds like it'll be a great time." I place my hands on the desk, bracing myself. "I can't wait."

We hang up the phone, and I dial Maria's number, and I squeal into the phone. "He wants me to go *with* him to his movie premiere!"

"That's great. It sounds like he's ready to share you with the world," she points out.

"Oh, wow. What am I going to wear?" I instantly start flipping through my Rolodex, looking for my makeover masters—the ones I send my clients to. "What does someone wear when her boyfriend wants to share her with the whole world?"

"I don't know, but I think this calls for some serious shopping. Let's go this weekend, since I'm assuming we won't be hanging out with Preston and Charlie." Silence fills the line. "Have you talked with either of them?"

"No." I really don't want to talk about them right now. I don't want them to ruin my high. "Shopping sounds like a fantastic idea."

Alexander wants to share me with the world! My heart starts to beat faster as I think about it—everyone knowing that I'm his girlfriend. Or at least his date for a very important premiere. We'll see what Preston and Charlie have to say about me being average once they see a picture of me with Alexander!

Two hours later, Clara sits across from me, her hands hugging her Coach purse tightly to her stomach. A big, excited smile stretches across her face. I have known Clara for five years now. She was one of my first clients and is my most regular one. Maria thinks she's crazy for wanting to meet so many celebrities, and even more so for paying to meet them. But I know differently. Clara is your everyday girl-next-door. Not too pretty, though not unattractive either. She drives an average middle-class car and lives in Pasadena, your average middle-class suburb. She has three school-age children and is a stay-at-home mom. Her way of having fun is meeting celebrities. Meetings with Clara are straightforward. She wants to be acknowledged. A simple everyday interaction with a stranger she'll never see again is enough to make her happy.

My success is, in large part, due to Clara. Not only is she a repeat customer, but many of my past clients were sent my way by her. I think back to how we first met. Maria and I were in Pasadena for one of our nights out with Charlie and Preston. We had stopped at a grocery store to pick up some wine, and Clara was in front of us, her three children in tow. At first I hadn't paid her much attention. She was just a woman in a grocery store who was reading a tabloid as her children begged and pleaded for some candy. Then Maria started talking to her.

"These tabloids make you think the streets are crawling with celebrities," she commented, a slight southern drawl coming through. "But I've been living here for eight years and have yet to even *see* one in person."

Maria inconspicuously glanced at me and nudged my elbow. "Really?" she asked. "I've met quite a few."

Clara's eyes grew wide. "You must be very lucky then. I'd give anything to call my friends back home and tell them I saw someone famous."

"Well, you should meet my friend, Olivia, then." Maria grabbed me and wedged me between the two of them.

"Oh?" Her eyebrows crinkled. "Are you a celebrity?"

"No." I looked around to make sure no one was listening, glared at Maria out of the corner of my eye, and then explained to Clara what

I do. Maria knew exactly what she was doing. One week later, Clara was sitting in my office and we were coming up with a plan for her to meet Gregory Foster, the star of her favorite sit-com.

Today I am excited to hear who she wants to meet. I ask her about the family and get all the small talk out of the way before we delve into our upcoming adventure.

She brushes a chunk of highlighted hair out of her eyes. "All my friends from Atlanta keep calling me because they absolutely love that movie *The Champion*."

Hmm. Alexander was in that. My mind briefly strays back to my conversation with him this morning, leaving me distracted. I wonder who he took to that premiere.

She continues to look at me, expectantly.

"Okay." I'm not sure what she's getting at. There are about ten big name celebrities in that movie.

"Okay, so—" She continues to look at me. "I want to meet Alexander Young!" she squeals then gathers herself and folds her well-manicured hands in her lap, waiting for my response.

I am speechless. I knew the day would come when someone would request Alexander, but I kept thinking I'd figure it out when it happens. And here it is—happening. And happening with my best client.

Clara's eyes narrow and the excitement wanes from her expression. "You know, the really good-looking one with the muscular arms and that sexy jawline?" The enthusiasm builds again in her voice as she describes him.

I still can't conjure up words to respond.

"You do know who Alexander Young is, right?" Her eyebrows raise, and her smile tightens.

"Yes, of course I know who—" My mouth stops moving. I can't bring myself to say his name. As if he will hear me if I do. "Who *he* is. I've just never arranged a meeting with, uh, *for* him."

"That's okay! Look," she enthuses as she pulls a file out of her purse and hands it to me. "I've been doing my homework!"

I take the file from her. She certainly has done her homework. There are tabloid clippings, newspaper articles, pages printed from the

Internet, and handwritten notes, all neatly stacked together. I try to buy myself some time to come up with something to say. I slowly go from one sheet of paper to another, not really looking at them at all.

"When can we do it? I was thinking if we can swing it, maybe before my trip back home?"

"Clara." I'm still at a loss for words. I have to come up with something. "I don't know. All of the celebrities I've arranged for you to meet have been celebrities I'm really familiar with. I just don't know enough about...*him* to comfortably arrange a meeting."

"But you arrange meetings with new celebrities all the time," she reasons. "I'm sure it'll be fine; you've always come through for me before." She shrugs her shoulders.

I am trying to weigh my options here, but my brain is working much too fast to create anything that resembles a coherent thought.

"Please?" she beams. "I could be your guinea pig—"

I have no choice. "Fine," I say, folding my hands together, trying to hide the shaking.

"Yes!" She jumps a little in her seat.

"I will look through these papers tonight," I interrupt her, "and see what I can come up with. I'll let you know tomorrow."

She throws her purse over her shoulder and bounces out the door.

Once she is gone, I lock the door and flip open the file. I'm astounded at the volume of information she has, a lot of it from the same sources I use. What's even more shocking is that most of it is not exactly true. Sure, his whereabouts are accurate, but the personal stuff is just so far *off.*

It occurs to me that I have never read anything about him in any of the tabloids that I read on a daily basis. Maybe I've been trying to ignore the fact that he's a celebrity. Or maybe I've been afraid of what I will find. But here it is before me, and now I have to read it.

Or do I?

I should call Clara right now and tell her I can't help her. I'll say that...What will I say? That I'm crazy in love with him and don't want to share him with anyone, that I refuse to arrange the meeting? Or should I tell her that he's my boyfriend, and he has absolutely no idea what I do for a living and arranging this meeting might completely, utterly ruin the relationship beyond repair? The truth hurts.

I suck my lower lip between my teeth and start to chew. I tap my fingers on the desk on either side of the file that lays, in front of me, invitingly open. Maybe if I treat it as a regular case, I can pull it off. I've done meetings before where I'm nowhere in sight. I've coached Clara so many times that she would be the perfect candidate. I let out a big, regretful sigh, the kind that you breathe when you know you're about to do something that will get you in trouble, and I read the clippings she's brought me.

"Alexander Young dines at a local Thai restaurant with his buddy Al Pacino." There isn't a picture, but the writer goes on to describe the very restaurant where Alexander picked up dinner on the night we went to the Griffith Park Observatory. On the other hand, I clearly remember a conversation we had that same night with those fans. He said that he's never met Al Pacino, though hopes to work with him someday.

"Alexander Young Fights Sister Over Custody of French Poodle, Loses." Ha. I guess that explains why I've never met the dog...or heard him mention any sister. I make a note for myself to not rely much on that tabloid anymore.

"Alexander hides his new girlfriend. The couple has been seen around town, holding hands and dining together. No one has been able to identify the new love interest or photograph her. Word around town is it's getting serious."

Oh. No. How did this never occur to me? I should've been reading the tabloids since our first date on the lookout for something like this. I can't be seen with Alexander! Especially not by my clients, who—I can't forget—read the tabloids every day. If Clara were to find a picture of me with Alexander, she would think I'm a big fake...and so would everyone she knows.

This trip down the red carpet with Alexander isn't looking like such a great idea anymore. How can I be his date and not have pictures taken with him?

Once I'm seen with him, I'm one of *them* to my clients. My entire business, along with my anonymity, would be destroyed. I can't arrange an everyday meeting in which my client isn't viewed as a fan if I'm seen as a celebrity. I frantically start flipping through the papers to see if there is any way Clara could have seen me.

Nothing.

I flip open my laptop and type in "Alexander Young's girlfriend." I get some website that lists all the celebrities he's dated but no mention of a *mysterious girl* anywhere. Just a tugging feeling in my heart that I didn't need to know who he dated before me.

If I back out of arranging this meeting with Clara, someone else someday soon will ask for Alexander. I can put him on my list of celebrities I don't arrange meetings with because they are known for, well, less than favorable behavior, but no one would ever believe that about the guy who won Fan Favorite at the last awards show. And if I turn down Clara, she won't be back, nor will her friends. I would risk losing this business that I've worked so hard for.

But if I arrange this meeting I could risk losing *him*.

Unless…I'm very careful. And that is how I've stayed in business all these years, by being careful. As I stare at the file gripped tightly in my hands, I realize there may be a way out of this. What if I arrange this meeting but use only the information that Clara provided me? Then I wouldn't, technically, be betraying Alexander because I wouldn't be using any information that wasn't public knowledge. That's it.

I have to make this meeting simple, and I have to do it quick. I grab a post-it and jot down, "Clara-Alexander: info for pending meeting," and I plant it onto the folder that's full of everything she has gathered on her own about Alexander.

Now if only I could figure out how to attend a red carpet event where he's going to share me with the world without actually getting photographed.

CHAPTER
20

T HE NEXT MORNING I SIT staring at my phone, chewing on the edge of my cup from the coffee I finished drinking thirty minutes ago. I have to call Clara, but I'm having a hard time believing what I had convinced myself of yesterday.

I take a deep breath. Then another. I plant my feet squarely on the floor. I mindlessly put the cup in the trash and take another deep breath. Then I dial.

"Hello?" Clara answers instantly.

I have no patience for small talk today and get right to it.

"Hey, Clara, I have a plan. Are you available tomorrow morning?" I spurt out.

"Wow. That is soon. But, umm, yes. Yes! What's the plan?"

"Okay, you're going to have to go it alone because I have another client I've been planning to meet with, but it looks like this will be your only opportunity before you leave for your trip." Although I thought this through at least a hundred times, there is a tugging at my heart that this isn't the right thing to do.

"Okay," she sings, "not a problem! I'm sure that with your instructions I will be just fine."

"It looks like he gets his car washed every Friday morning, according to an Internet source. And another source says he's a regular at—"

My other line starts ringing. "I'm sorry, Clara, can I put you on hold for a minute?"

I click over to my other line, and my heart slips all the way down to the bottom of my stomach.

"Hey," Alexander breathes into the phone.

"I was just thinking about you," I blurt out before I can stop myself. I can hear him smile through the phone.

"Looks like my schedule has cleared up tomorrow. I was thinking if you're free, we could go to the Huntington Gardens. I can pick you up at nine?"

"I'd love to," I surrender. Then I click back to Clara.

I pick up right where I left off. "He's a regular at Sunset Carwash on Sunset, just past Fairfax." And I read her the plan as I had laid it out the night before. "You need to be there at nine a.m."

We hang up the phone and, just like that, the decision I tossed and turned over all night, is easily decided for me. I choose Alexander.

CHAPTER
21

AT 9:02 EXACTLY, I OPEN my door to a confident knock. Even though we've been dating for a couple of months now and have seen each other often, his effect on me never changes. My heart races, the whole world slows, an involuntary smile spreads across my face. When I look into his eyes that are smiling back at me, everything in the world is right. He leans in and kisses my cheek.

"You look beautiful," he says with a raised eyebrow.

I swish the skirt of my striped summer dress and kid, "Oh, this old thing?"

He walks in and makes himself comfortable in my green chair. Since he has been coming over more often,

I've gotten into the habit of only bringing home the work that is really necessary and stashing it in the lower left corner of my closet, behind a fluffy winter coat.

He puts his hand out for me to grab and then pulls me onto the arm of the chair. He wraps his arm around me. "You smell delicious." He tugs me closer until I'm sitting on his lap.

"Thank you," I manage to squeak out, my heart still racing.

He leans in and kisses me. His lips fit perfectly against mine, his hand brushes my hair behind my shoulder and falls away.

"I think we'd better go," he whispers throatily. I nod my head in agreement, even though staying home with Alexander sounds like a wonderful plan as well.

Downstairs he opens the car door for me. As I climb in, I notice how clean his car is and the faint smell of new-car air freshener. Looks like that piece of tabloid information is true, at least it is for today.

"I hope you're not missing anything important at work today," he says as he starts the car.

"No. Not a thing," I reply honestly.

We weave down the freeway, chatting easily as we sit in traffic and make our way across town. After about an hour, we pull up to a large gate that opens onto a barren parking lot. He gives his name and shows a card to the security guard, and we are waved though. The droopy tree that shades our parking spot sways in the breeze as we walk toward the main building. There are not a lot of people around, and I'm wondering if this might be the red carpet event he had invited me to. But as we approach the window, I notice other people with cards similar to Alexander's. He shows his card again, and we are given stickers to wear that read, "member event."

My curiosity must be showing because he gives me that sexy half-smile again. "It's an art preview that doesn't open to the public for another week. I thought you might enjoy it." We follow the few people strolling across the grass fields to a tall white building.

He pushes the door open and a stream of soothing jazz floats around us and out the door. Pictures of Ella Fitzgerald, Count Basie, and John Coltrane hang on the walls among frames filled with other jazz greats. The center of the room has easels, each of them holding up some colorful, emotive piece of art.

There's a big, smooth, city moon silhouetting a man in a white suit who is playing a trombone. Another made with thick, chunky brushstrokes of men in bright suits tapping the drum, plucking the bass. Some with paint dripping, blurring so that it's hard to tell where the man stops and the instrument begins. All portraying the jazz I grew up with. I must've been standing there without moving for a few minutes because the next thing I hear is Alexander whispering in my ear, as sexy as a serenading songstress, "I guess this means you like it?"

We flow from painting to painting, sharing memories they trigger, bobbing our heads to the jazz that's humming through the air, his warm hand on the small of my back, guiding me gently through the room. When we reach the end of the exhibit, we find our way out and wander through the gardens, holding hands, hunting through the roses, reading every label for names of family members and friends. We find a bench to sit on near a tranquil pond. Just as he leans over to put his arm around me, I hear my phone beep three times. Voicemail.

"Do you need to check that?" he asks.

"No," I say, "it can wait." I know exactly who it is.

When we return to the car, ready to leave before the gardens are opened to the public, I quickly glance at my phone as he slides into the seat next to me. I see the words, "voicemail from Clara."

"I really don't mind if you need to check that. I know I sort of kidnapped you from work this morning."

"Really," I insist, "it can wait."

He drives home with his hand on my leg, and I am just giddy. He occasionally runs his thumb softly across the top of my knee, and I nearly explode. When he pulls up in front of my apartment I don't want to get out. He walks me to my door.

"I know this is kind of last minute, but I was wondering if you want to have dinner tonight?" he bashfully asks.

"I think I can make it," I whisper back.

He leans in and kisses me and then he is gone. I float back into my apartment and decide to work from home.

Trying to bring myself back to reality, I focus on this morning's meeting. Or rather this morning's *missed* meeting. I dig through my closet and pull out my work cache, flipping through the files until I come across the one that says "Alexander Young" across the tab. I work on my story for Clara and then brace myself to listen to her message.

"Hi, Olivia. I think I may have been at the wrong car wash, or maybe I was looking for a different car, or maybe he has someone take his car to get washed because there definitely was no sign of Alexander Young anywhere. And I'm pretty sure he wouldn't be able to get very far without being noticed. Looks like I do still really need you to be there after all. I leave for Georgia next week. Maybe we can work something out when I get back? Give me a call."

Thank you! Clara thinks it's her fault she didn't find Alexander. The horrible thought, though, that's been lingering is still there. This may have bought me some time, but what happens when she gets back from Georgia? I can only keep setting up fake meetings for so long before she figures out something is going on,

I grab a new post-it and jot down, "Plan for next meeting" and stick it on top of the folder. I'll have to come up with a way to avoid another meeting later.

That night we have a quiet dinner at one of Alexander's favorite restaurants, Canelé. It's a small, romantic out-of-the-way kind of place. As dinner ends, he gets very quiet. There is a nervousness about him, just like the other day on the phone when he asked me to go to the red carpet event with him.

"Well," he starts. He leans his elbows on the table and rests the side of his chin on his intertwined knuckles.

I smile back.

"I was thinking that maybe we could go back to my place," he says sexily, softly. "If you want to, that is."

I love seeing how he is afraid of me rejecting him. What a thought. I take a breath and count to five. Not because I'm angry, but because

I don't want to scream YES! like a desperate teenager before he even finishes asking the question. At that, we hop in his car and zoom down the road.

We enter a gated community and drive for a few more minutes before coming to another gate, amid a long hedge. He pushes a button in his car, and the gates swing open, leading us up a rounded drive. He parks and opens my door for me. There is a large pool sprawling across the yard. It is so camouflaged among palm trees, waterfalls, and rocks bordering the grass that it looks more like an oasis. There are a few pool chairs thoughtfully placed around the yard, each with their own carefully disguised palm tree umbrella. On the other side of the car is the actual house—a two-story Spanish-inspired building. There is a large arch with two enormous wooden doors underneath. On either side of the arch there are balconies with mission-style wooden rails overlooking the pool area.

He opens the door and motions for me to enter. Inside, his home looks comfortable, like I could plop down on a sofa and no one would mind. Overstuffed leather chairs surround an antique-looking mantle above a fireplace. The Spanish tile neatly laid in the floors is partly covered with lush white carpeting, the kind you want to run your bare feet through. He leads me past the dining room that's filled with a large table, made from an enormous old door, and upholstered chairs, lined neatly along its edge. We pass the kitchen door where I catch a glimpse of an expansive room with engraved dark cupboards and shiny counters. Finally we come to a sitting room. He leads me to a comfortable sofa and spins me around before I land softly in the middle.

"Can I get you a glass of wine?" he asks.

"Yes, please." I could use a little something to calm my nerves.

He retreats toward the kitchen and leaves me to make myself at home. I glance around to distract myself from what the rest of the evening may hold, noticing the pictures he has framed on his wall. A young boy, could be Alexander, many years ago, holding hands with an older girl standing in front of a dinosaur. An old black-and-white photograph taken on someone's wedding day. The groom is tall and serious, the bride is beautiful, a big smile glowing on her face.

In the corner of the room, almost hidden, there is a shelf. On top of it sits his three SAG awards, two framed academy nominations, and his Golden Globe. I can still hear him in the kitchen, so I walk over and pick up the Golden Globe. I've always been curious about how heavy they are. I resist the urge to give a pretend acceptance speech before gently putting it back down.

The center of attention on the shelf is a framed picture of a car in front of a car wash. Not just any car wash, but the one I sent Clara to today. I recognize the unique sign with palm trees sprouting up here and there. A sinking feeling hits.

"I hope red is fine," he says as he enters the room, jolting me back to the present.

"Perfect," I say. *Just like you*, I think.

He sits on the sofa and pulls me closer, his deep green eyes intently gazing into mine. Afraid my feelings will get the better of me, I turn to the photos.

"Is that you?"

"Me and my cousin," he says. "That was our last family vacation before she went off to college."

"And who's the happy couple?" I joke.

"My mom's mom and dad. They had just gotten married and were leaving for America the next day. My grandmother was thrilled. My grandfather was a little nervous."

"And the car?"

"My grandfather's car," he interrupts me. "It was the first car he bought after he moved here. It was his pride and joy." He beams as he speaks of his grandfather. "He bought it from the car wash owner's son. Every Friday he would take it to get washed. The owner's son would come out and wash it himself. I think he was a little sad that he had to sell it. My grandfather used to take me with him every once in a while, and we would have ice cream, and he'd tell me stories about back home."

"Now it's your car?" I ask.

"He left it to me when he was too old to drive. Every Friday he would have me take it to get washed. He said the owner's son would want to see it. He's still there, you know."

"The owner's son?" I ask.

"Yeah. He's the owner now. I still take it on Fridays. If I can't make it, I have some one take it for me."

I want to hide. Not only did I try to arrange a meeting for a client with my boyfriend for money, but I exploited a family tradition. Suddenly, right then and there, reality hits me. I have to tell him. I have to tell Alexander that I get paid to interrupt the daily lives of celebrities for the benefit of my paying clients. I have to tell him that I read tabloids daily as if they are the Bible. I have to tell him that I have no respect for his or his colleagues' privacy. I have to.

"Are you okay?" he asks.

"Yeah," I take a deep breath, ready to tell all. But those eyes distract me. That jawline makes me start to daydream. That curl of his hair makes me forget what I want to say. What I *need* to say.

He senses my readiness, leans in, and kisses me. Before I know it, I'm wrapped up in his arms, our legs tangle together on the sofa. He slowly makes his way down my neck, and I am lost.

"Should we go upstairs?" he asks throatily.

I nod. And any thoughts of what I should do in reality completely disappear.

CHAPTER
22

I WAIT, LEANING AGAINST THE ARMCHAIR in my living room, bouncing my leg up and down. The piazza is an especially vibrant shade of green today with red, yellow, and pink flowers peeking out from behind the leaves. I glance at my freshly manicured nails and let the minutes slowly drag by until Alexander picks me up.

A dark town car pulls up in front of the apartment, and I see my neighbor step outside her front door, pretending to grab a breath of fresh air. Alexander steps out of the car, and my knees go weak. Seeing him on a regular day sends my heart into overdrive, but today, I can hardly keep from pulling him against me and not letting go.

As he reaches my front door I open it, and we just stand there, staring at each other.

"You look amazing." He slowly shakes his head. "You'd better be careful or you may land yourself on the cover of a magazine." He chuckles at his joke, not realizing that this really is one of my biggest fears, not that I'll be on the cover of a magazine, but that I'll be photographed with Alexander. And that my career will come to a screeching halt.

To hide my discomfort, I stand and pose with my hands on my hips, and then slowly turn, making sure to pause when my back is to him, and I give a little wink over my bare shoulder. He steps forward and puts his arm around me, resting it on the small of my back, which happens to be bare in this dress that Maria and I spent hours deciding on.

He leans down and kisses my neck. "That reminds me," he whispers, "I got you a little something." He hands me a long, black velvety box. Trying to steady my hands, I place the box on my side table as I swivel it open.

"Alexander," I whisper back, "I don't know what to say! It's beautiful!" He undoes the clasp and slips the gold chain around my neck. The blue sapphire in the center plays off the hint of blue in my dark gray dress, while the encircling diamonds bring out the subtle crystal detailing throughout my gown.

He steps back and looks at me, smiling. The vein in his temple beats, and I steady myself on the doorframe. He takes my hand and leads me to the car.

Our ride to the Westwood movie theater is rather silent, with Alexander's hand on my knee, which is bare beside the slit of my dress.

"Are you nervous?" I ask. "About seeing the finished movie?"

He shrugs. "I just don't want to let anyone down."

He is about to attend an event in which he will most likely be surrounded by hundreds of his fans flooding the streets, trying to catch a glimpse of him (the same fans who could potentially be knocking on my door someday), and he's worried about letting people down.

It strikes me in that moment just how lucky I am. It doesn't matter how I met Alexander; it only matters that I have. And really, if my job could help even one of my clients come close to feeling what I'm feeling right now, then what I do is worth the risk. How can Alexander not understand that? I'm sure he will. That is, when I get around to telling him what it is that I do.

The driver opens Alexander's door, and a confident woman, wearing a black pantsuit and red shoes, is standing there ready to greet him. He turns to me. "Are you ready?"

"Yes," I say, but inside I'm screaming *no*!

He slides out of the car and, seconds later, my door opens, and the driver's hand appears to help me out. Before I even step onto the curb, a woman is vigorously shaking my hand.

"Nice to meet you, Ms. Fowler," she sputters. "I'm Priscilla, assistant publicist. I'll be taking care of you today." She pushes her thin and stylish glasses up her nose.

I smile and nod, unsure of exactly what is going on. Alexander leans over and kisses me on the cheek.

"I have to go take care of a few things," he apologizes. "Priscilla will take care of you while I'm gone." He kisses me on the cheek again, and the woman with the red shoes glances up from her clipboard and whisks him away.

I'm left standing there, awkwardly, in my formal dress without a date. In fact, I'm feeling a little like my prom date just stood me up. I may be able to arrange meetings with celebrities, but rubbing elbows with them is a completely different experience.

I turn to Priscilla for guidance and notice that she is watching Alexander walk away with Ms. Red Shoes. With one eyebrow raised, her pen tucked into the corner of her mouth, and her gaze a little lower than I prefer, I decide not to trust her. Finally, she turns to me, only I notice that her smile isn't quite as big as before. Nor is her interest in me.

"I'll show you where to wait for Mr. Young," she states matter-of-factly. "There's a room right over here." She starts to walk in the opposite direction from where Alexander went.

"But shouldn't we—" I start, a little mousier than I would've liked. I try again, louder. "Don't we need to go this way, toward the theater entrance?"

"No," she says without even turning around, "that's only for *important* people. You need to go in the back entrance. He'll find you…inside."

We walk away from the crowds who are huddling by the front entrance as a few girls scream, and then the crowd gets louder. I hear a few shouts of "Alexander, over here!" and even an "I love you, Alexander!!!" I assume he is walking down the red carpet. Without me.

We come to a white door, barely distinguishable from the white stucco wall of the theater, except for the words Emergency Exit written in large red letters across the top. This doesn't seem right. Although I've never actually been to a red carpet event, this is nothing like what I've heard. *Maybe Alexander wants to make sure I'm comfortable.* I'm sure he's picked up on my hesitation about being around celebrities, the way I always change the subject when they come up.

She pulls on the handle, and the door opens onto a dark hallway. I follow her, hesitantly, careful not to let my dress get caught as the door slams behind me. I slide my hand along the wall to help navigate the dark hall, following the click-click of Priscilla's heels. I hear her fiddling with some part of the door and briefly wonder if she's going to lead me to Alexander or if she plans to lock me in a dark closet somewhere, in hopes of taking my place in the soon-to-be-empty seat next to my date.

The door swings open and we are, thankfully, in the lobby, which is now crawling with guests.

"Here you go." She gestures in no direction in particular. "Just wait here, and I'll come get you in a bit." Before I have a chance to respond, she is lost in the crowd.

I stand as straight as I can and try to look like I belong, although I'm not really sure why I would be standing in a fancy theater lobby in a formal dress by myself, next to an old-fashioned popcorn machine. I glance around so it looks like I expect to see someone I know. And to think, I was worried about being photographed with Alexander. I'm beginning to think I'll be lucky if I get to sit with him.

It seems like hours pass, though I'm sure it's only twenty minutes or so. The crowd in the lobby is starting to thin out. Should I try to find my way to my seat? Surely he can't be that hard to find. He'd be in the front row. Or maybe not. Alexander doesn't like to put himself before others. Maybe he'd be in the back. But why would the star of a movie sit in the last row at his own premiere? Perhaps I should walk up and down the aisle looking for him. I take a few steps toward the double doors that lead to the seating area of the theater.

That's when I realize I don't have credentials of any sort. They're bound to throw me out if I'm wandering up and down the aisle. And when I tell them I'm Alexander's date? That would be a sure ticket out the door. So, instead, I slink back against the wall and hope to blend in with the wallpaper until Alexander finds me. *IF* Alexander finds me.

"Olivia?" A familiar voice comes from my right. But it's not Alexander. "I didn't know you were going to be here."

"Charlie?" I am just as surprised as he is. "What are you doing here?"

"One of my clients has a bit part in the movie and asked me to come with her to help, you know, publicize," he says. "Where's Alexander?"

I begin to blush. I'm not sure what to say, seeing as last time I saw Charlie we didn't leave on very good terms. At this point, what have I got to lose? "Well, ummm, that's a good question. I seem to have, ummmm, lost him."

"You lost your date? The star of the movie?" He chuckles. I can tell by his warm smile there are no hard feelings. "I'd think he'd be pretty hard to lose."

"Red Shoe lady whisked him away through one door, and Priscilla brought me in through the emergency exit where all the unimportant people enter, then—"

"Wait," he interrupts, "Priscilla? Jane's assistant?"

I nod, assuming Jane is Alexander's publicist.

"She brought you in through the emergency exit?" He starts laughing.

"Yes." I'm beginning to think I was lied to. "Isn't that where everyone that's…What's so funny?"

Charlie is in full-laughter mode now.

"I'm sorry," he manages to squeeze out between laughs. "Priscilla Godzilla seems to have it out for you."

My face is serious now. My hands are on my hips. Charlie seems to wrangle in the laughter. He reaches out his arm and rests it on my shoulder.

"That door over there." He points to a set of double doors not twenty feet from the main entrance. "That is where you were supposed to come in. And that part of the lobby over there is where you're supposed to wait for your date."

My jaw drops. *Priscilla, that little weasel, is most definitely after my man.*

"Come on." Charlie puts his arm around me. "I'll help you find Alexander."

We head over to the end of the lobby. I see lots of celebrities from the movie, all standing with their dates but no Alexander. Priscilla is nearby, chatting with other publicist assistants; she quickly scuttles away before I have a chance to make eye contact with her.

"You look great, by the way," Charlie starts. "I'm really glad you're here. I guess I didn't realize you two were going public."

"Thanks, Charlie." I just knew he would come around to my relationship with Alexander. "I'm glad you understand. Maybe you can talk some sense into Preston."

Charlie looks into my eyes and opens his mouth, about to say something, when…

"Olivia!" Alexander exclaims. "I've been looking all over for you! Where have you been? Priscilla said you walked off, and she couldn't find you."

Charlie and I give each other knowing glances. Just then, a tall blond woman who I vaguely recognize from a cancelled television show calls Charlie over to introduce him to some other tall blond woman.

"See you later," he says as he leans over and hugs me goodbye, and then nods to Alexander.

"Thanks, Charlie." I finger wave and give him a small, knowing grin.

"Charlie?" Alexander asks. His eyebrows crinkle. "*That's* Preston's friend? What's he doing here?"

"He's a publicist." I cock my head to the side. "Haven't I mentioned that?"

A man at the front of the lobby catches Alexander's attention and motions for us to head into the theater.

"Looks like it's time to go in." Grabbing my hand, he takes two steps and then stops. He looks directly at me, and he looks nervous. "Promise me something?"

"What?" I smile at him.

"Promise you'll tell me what you think, for real." He pulls me closer and lowers his voice. "Everyone here will say they like it, to me. That's how this business works. But I want the truth. I want to know what parts you love and what parts you hate. All of it. And only the truth."

"Of course." I'm floored that my opinion means so much to him. My heart warms as his look of concern turns to a calm smile. He leans in and kisses me, this time on the lips.

As we start to walk into the theater, I realize that the entire lobby is watching us.

The crowd erupts into applause. Some people toward the front stand up, followed by some more. I hop to my feet and join in the clapping. Soon the entire theater is filled with standing, clapping people. Alexander is smiling. A tall man in a dark green suit in front of us turns around and congratulates him. Alexander says thank you quietly as he stands and shakes his hand, and then says what a great job the director did and mentions some of the actors by name.

As the theater begins to empty, Alexander stays by his seat. The entire crowd stops on their way out to shake his hand and tell him what a great movie it was. Every few minutes, he puts his arm around me, introducing me to people here and there, mostly celebrities. It occurs to me that I hadn't thought about work once tonight. The working part of me would have been taking mental notes of all the celebrities here, who they are with and how they are acting toward people they don't know.

"Olivia," Alexander's voice brings me back to the present, "This is Ryan Scott. We've done a few movies together, and he's thinking about getting involved in my charity program."

"Its nice to meet you," Ryan says as he extends a hand to me. "This is my girlfriend, Sarah."

There, right in front of me is my former client, Sarah. I flash back to all those hours we spent sitting in a Starbucks waiting for Ryan to walk in. Of all the scenarios I had gone through in my head about how this night might go wrong, not once did it occur to me that I could run into a former client *with* a celebrity I had helped her meet.

"Nice to meet you." Sarah smiles, looking intensely into my eyes.

"Yes," I catch on, "so nice to meet both of you."

A man from across the aisle grabs Alexander and Ryan's attention momentarily. Sarah leans in and whispers, "It's about time, Olivia. I always wondered why you didn't use your gift for catching one of your own." She pulls away from me before I have a chance to respond—to tell her that no, I didn't *catch* Alexander. Ryan grabs her hand, and they disappear into the crowd.

Alexander leans in and kisses me on the cheek.

"You doing all right?" he asks.

"I'm doing great." I lean in and kiss him back. "Never been better."

I know my secret is safe with Sarah. After all, we both have the same secret to keep.

"I just have a few more pictures to take, and then we can head out."

"Okay." I'm beginning to see how this works. "I'll wait over here for you."

"Really?" He starts chuckling. "I'd really rather you come with me. I mean, you are my date and all."

Pictures? Not pictures! Think quick, Olivia!

"Sure," I stammer, trying to buy time. "I just need to run to the ladies room. I think I shed a few tears during your performance, and I'd like to freshen up."

"You look beautiful." He stares at me. "I promise."

He grabs my hand and pulls me to the lobby. I brace myself for the wall of cameras I am sure is on the other side of the doors. Do I smile and look happy, making the best of the situation? Or should I keep trying to distance myself? Maybe if I stand far enough away people won't think I'm really *with* him.

We pass through the doors and, to my surprise, there are only two photographers. I try to step away from Alexander, but he puts his arm around my waist and pulls me closer. I try again to pull away, and this time he lets me go, and I end up stumbling, landing right in the arms of the cameraman.

"Oh!" I cry. "I'm so sorry! You're not going to sue me for assaulting you, right?" I try to make a joke out of my little disaster, hoping this photographer has a sense of humor. No such luck.

"No, Sheila." He puckers his face, making it hard to understand his Australian accent. "That's the paparazzi who does that. I'm Jobe Graff. I take real pictures."

Jobe Graff! He's almost as famous as the celebrities he photographs! He's won the International Photography Award and has two (not one, but TWO) Pulitzer Prizes.

"How are you, Jobe?" Alexander asks. "This is my date, Olivia."

Jobe pauses, looking confused. Then, without missing a beat, he says, "Olivia, why don't you stand with Alexander. Let's capture some memories here."

Automatically I find myself at his side. Wiggling as close as I can possibly get without making a scene. I smile big, resting my hand on his chest. Alexander tilts his head toward mine and caresses my shoulder. He turns and kisses my forehead.

"What a moment!" Jobe exclaims.

Before I know what I'm doing, my lips are finding Alexander's, and my arms are wrapping tighter around him. I can't help myself. When will I ever have the opportunity to be photographed by Jobe Graff again?

After our kiss, he pulls away and smiles intently at me. I see his vein up close now. My heart skips a beat.

"Let's get going," he whispers hoarsely into my ear.

We head out the door and to the car.

CHAPTER
23

I GLANCE OVER AT THE CLOCK on the wall of my office and then back down at the tabloid on my desk. I reread the same paragraph for the fifth time. I glance back at the clock. I check my hair and makeup in the mirror, again. Maybe I shouldn't have worn these black slacks with this turquoise blouse. I should've worn the beige one. No, I should've worn jeans.

I sit back down at my desk and take out a pen to jot down some notes but find myself looking at the clock and clicking the pen repeatedly. This is crazy. I was calmer before the first time Alexander and I met for coffee.

I suppose I didn't have as much to risk then. Or at least I didn't know how much I had to risk. But today, it has to be perfect. And I have no control over the outcome. What if Maria and Alexander don't like each other? Will I have to choose? No, neither of them would make me do that, I don't think. What if Maria picks up on something that I've been too blind to see? What if she sees that he doesn't like me? Maybe it's all one-sided.

I am going to lose my mind if I keep this up. How can this meeting be getting to me so much when I arrange meetings with normal people and celebrities all the time? And I never *really* know how those will turn out either.

That's it! I need to think of this just like I would a meeting I've arranged. Maria is a normal person and Alexander is a celebrity after all. The only difference is Maria is my best friend, more like a sister, really. And Alexander knows about the meeting. And is basically my boyfriend. Basically my wonderful boyfriend. With whom things have been going really well.

So well that I can't believe it's been four months since we first met for coffee. All those nights we stayed up late, talking about everything—what we wanted to be when we grew up, where we spent our summers as kids, when we had our first kisses. It's hard to believe we haven't known each other for very long.

Then it hits me, the reason I'm so nervous about introducing Alexander to Maria. I've done such a good job separating my personal life from my work life since I met Alexander. The thought of combining the two is petrifying.

The Olivia that arranges meetings knows everything there is to know about celebrities. She can track them down and arrange a dream meeting with even those who are most reclusive. They don't make her nervous. She has her act together, even under the most stressful situations.

The Olivia that Alexander knows doesn't read tabloids. She doesn't hang around the Hollywood crowd or even care where they hang out. She has no interest in being famous or in famous people. She has a very normal life.

While Maria isn't exactly *work*, she has been my guinea pig for a lot of test meetings. What if one of those stories accidentally comes out in conversation? What if he mentions my work? Will Maria know how to answer his questions? What if she let's something slip that gets him wondering?

STOP! I close my eyes and steady my hands on the desk. It will be fine. I am introducing Maria, my best friend of forever, who knows me better than anyone and would never let anything about my secret slip, to my boyfriend, who seems to really like me.

I glance at the clock. Maria will be here any second, and we will be on our way to meet Alexander. There is a knock at the door. "Come in!" I yell to Maria.

Fifteen minutes later we are headed down Interstate 10 toward The Ivy, an upscale Beverly Hills restaurant.

"Are you nervous?" Maria asks.

"I was. But not really anymore." I look at her. "Should I be?"

"Of course not. What is there to worry about?"

"I don't know."

"You do know. Just tell me." She pauses. "Are you worried I'll accidentally tell him about your work?"

I don't want to offend her. I know she would never do that on purpose, though she does like attention.

"Of course not. Maybe. Not on purpose." I try to find the right words to describe how I'm feeling. "I just know how much you love telling stories about our past. And how much people like to hear them. So I might be a little afraid that you'll get carried away and—"

"I won't. I promise. I'm here for you." She looks intently at me. "What else is bothering you?"

I squint my eyes, briefly glancing at her.

"I can tell there's something. You already have a scarf on. Usually you spill during meals, not before them, unless you're really nervous." She raises her eyebrows, waiting for me to answer.

"It's just...what if it's all my imagination? What if I'm way more into him than he's into me?"

"Hmmm." She thinks for a moment. "Maybe."

I whip my head around to her—my eyes fill with panic, my heart rate increasing.

"But I doubt that's true," she adds. "From all that you've told me about him, it sounds like he's absolutely crazy about you. Why wouldn't he be, Liv? You're a smart, beautiful woman who runs her own successful business."

I raise my eyebrows, eyes widening.

"Okay, fine, the business part needs a little spin. But really, you are an amazing, caring, and fun person. Everybody knows that. Oh!" she yells, pointing to the side of the street, "parking spot!"

I drive to the curb, and we both pull down the visors and check ourselves in the mirror one more time.

"It's going to be fine. I promise." She turns to get out of the car, but right before she opens the door, she whispers to me, "So I shouldn't mention that soccer league I played in for you, right?"

I cock my head to the side and narrow my eyes as she starts laughing and slides out of the car.

In The Ivy, we walk up to the hostess. She looks at us, without smiling, raising her eyebrows as if asking, "Can I help you?"

"We have reservations for three, under Fowler, Olivia," I tell her.

She scans the list in front of her. Then suddenly her attitude changes. "Yes, the rest of your party is already here. Right this way."

Maria leans over and whispers, "The perks of dating one of the most famous men on the planet, right?"

I smile back at her.

The hostess leads us to a small table on the patio where Alexander sits waiting for us. When he sees us, he rises. The waitress leaves the menus on the table and walks away. Alexander comes over and gives me a huge hug. Then he plants a big kiss on my cheek and looks into my eyes. I guess it was just my nerves getting the best of me.

"Hi. You look beautiful." He gives me one of his irresistible grins and then kisses me again, this time on the lips. Then he turns to Maria.

"Alexander, this is Maria," I assert.

"Maria. It's so nice to finally meet you." He reaches both his hands out and envelops her hand between his. "Olivia has told me so much about you; I feel like we're already friends."

"It's so nice to meet you too," she squeaks out. I've never seen Maria so taken aback by anyone, even a celebrity. I hope our little conversation about not telling any stories hasn't stifled her.

As we sit down, I try to think fast of how to break the ice.

"Olivia tells me you're really into roller skating." He gives Maria a soft smile and leans back in his chair, resting his hand on my knee.

Maria seems to snap to attention when he mentions her favorite hobby and the only thing she will ever ditch me for.

"Yes, I am an avid roller skater," she pipes in.

"How exactly does it work? Do you have teams? Does someone keep score? I've never had the chance to watch a roller derby."

Just like that, Maria has found her comfort zone and is off and running.

They get along wonderfully. She laughs at all his jokes. He is interested in what she is saying but not too interested. There isn't a hint of any story that relates to my work.

As the check arrives, I am starting to feel relief that I may actually make it through lunch without work being brought up. Just as I think I am in the clear, we hear a voice.

"Maria?" a man in jeans and a T-shirt with dark sunglasses says.

Maria turns her head. At first she looks as confused as I do. But then, as the man lifts his sunglasses, I see the terror spread across her face. Her jaw goes slack, the blood drains from her cheeks, and her eyes grow as large as quarters. A quick look at him, and I see exactly why.

"Daniel," she says.

"How are you? I haven't heard form you." He leans forward and tries to hug Maria, but she doesn't get up fast enough so she only half stands, making it a very awkward hug.

"I…oh, these are my friends. Alexander and—" she stops. I know she is remembering *never mention my name to a celebrity I've arranged for you to meet* because I did arrange her meeting with him all those months ago.

Alexander jumps in and, unknowingly, saves the day. "Daniel, good to see you, man."

"Alexander, how have you been?" he asks.

"Great. Just having lunch with my friends, Olivia," he starts as he puts his arm around my waist and leaves it there, "and Maria. Who you seem to know." He raises his eyebrows and looks at me, a little puzzled.

"Yeah, we met a while ago—" he begins. But before he can say anything incriminating, a tall skinny blond walks out of the restaurant behind him and interrupts.

"Are we ready to go, Danny?" she asks.

"Yes," he says to her. Then he turns to us. "Olivia, great to meet you. Alexander, I'll see you around."

As the blond starts walking away, Daniel turns to Maria. "It was good to see you," he says sincerely. "Don't be a stranger." Then he walks after the blond.

We sit, unsure of what to say, until Alexander breaks the silence. "Well, it sounds like Maria has been having some fun."

Maria and I both burst into laughter.

Alexander signs the check, and we all head out.

CHAPTER 24

I PULL UP TO THE GATE in front of Alexander's house and punch in the code. I hear a click before it swiftly slides across the driveway, letting me on the road. As I pull up behind his car, I see Alexander outside, bending over a bed of flowers. I get out of the car and walk up to him.

"Is everything okay?" I ask.

He jumps and turns his head to look at me. His grin implies I caught him in the middle of something. "I didn't hear you pull up." He walks over to me, one arm behind his back, and gives me a big hug, not letting go. I bury my face in his shoulder and take in the smell of him— part soap, part cologne, and the faintest hint of garlic, probably from lunch.

When I pull away, he holds a bunch of flowers out for me. "I was hoping to be done before you got here. I picked the ones I thought you'd like."

How sweet! My (probably) millionaire boyfriend could've sent someone to a florist, but, instead, with a pair of scissors, he got down on his hands and knees and picked what he thought I'd like best. He did a pretty good job too.

"Thank you." I lean in and kiss him on the lips. The kiss is warm and welcoming, like coming home after a long day. "They're beautiful."

"Let's go inside. I want to change before we head out." I follow him through the front doors and into the kitchen where he puts the flowers into a vase for the time being. Then he walks me to the sitting room, where I toss my purse on the table and lounge on the leather sofa. When he leaves me to go change, I can't help but think about the first time I was here. It seems like such a long time ago.

I glance at the pictures on the wall, and it hits me. Clara. The car. The car wash.

My secret.

How have I not yet told him? The longer I go without him knowing, the harder it will be to explain. Though maybe if I wait long enough for him to fall in love with me, then it won't matter. He'll just say, "Oh, really? You get paid to track celebrities and help people meet them? Without the celebrities knowing what's going on? No Problem. As long as we are together, that's all that matters."

Who am I kidding?

I hear him padding down the stairs. I can't tell him tonight. It doesn't feel right. But I will... soon. I just need a little more time to figure out *how.*

In the few minutes he was upstairs he has gone from scrubby guy in workout clothes holding garden flowers to sexy boyfriend in dark jeans and a super-soft polo shirt.

"Wow. Don't you look nice. I'm feeling a little underdressed here," I say because I am. Thinking we were going to have a casual night, I am suddenly regretting the jeans and crochet-hemmed long sleeve top, even though it took me twenty minutes to pick them out. I start to pull my hair from its ponytail when Alexander stops me.

"Wait, you look beautiful the way you are. In fact, you look amazing. And you're dressed perfectly for what I have in mind," he says.

I raise my eyebrows, skeptical that my hair in a ponytail would be acceptable anywhere that I could be seen with Alexander. What exactly does he have in mind?

"There is a bowling alley in the Roosevelt Hotel I've always wanted to try."

Bowling? He wants to go bowling? Bowling has never come up as an option when researching celebrities for my clients. But I guess that's what makes Alexander different, what makes *us* different.

I try to imagine how this will go. He will probably bowl a strike, and I will roll a gutter ball. I'll ask him for help. He'll stand behind me, his arms up against mine, guiding me where he wants me. Then he'll lean in and kiss my neck before we bowl a prefect strike. Yes, bowling sounds like fun. And it sounds like a place we can be ourselves and not worry about being interrupted.

"Bowling sounds great." I jump to my feet as he pulls me off the sofa and spins me around, landing us in a dip. He kisses my cheek and gently guides me back up. Then we walk, hand-in-hand out the door and to the car.

"This place is supposed to be amazing," he says as we ride the elevator to the second floor. "There are so few things in Los Angeles that have been around this long."

We walk into the Spare Room, and he is right. The bar area is beautiful with its curved, golden sofas and low tables, its art deco lighting and game tables. Tucked away between the length of the bar and enormous arched windows, overlooking the bright lights of the city, are two bowling lanes. Even the lanes look like art. Their shiny wooden floors in dual shades of immaculately polished wood. And the atmosphere. I feel hip and stylish just standing here.

Alexander gives his name to a lady holding a small book, and she nods him over to the bar. We each order a drink and wait for our lane to open.

Twenty minutes later, we are sipping the last of our drinks when the lady tells us it's our turn. As we are walking toward our lane, I'm not sure what comes over me, perhaps it's the drink or the confidence I've gained from merely standing in such a hip place, but I squeeze Alexander's hand. When he turns to see why, I let my impulses take over, and I pull him close, smothering his lips with mine.

Just as I feel him start to react, there is a bright flash. Then it's like the world goes into slow motion. I can feel his lips against mine, and then I feel the cool air from him pulling away. When I open my eyes, he is staring back at me with an expression I've never before seen, nor can I even begin to interpret.

Is he mad? I thought our relationship was out in the open. Ever since the premiere, he has been freely holding my hand in public, even leaning in for the occasional kiss when we're out and about. Then it occurs to me…aside from Jobe Graff, no one has photographed us together. I know this mostly because I've been scouring the tabloids and Internet to make sure my relationship with Alexander is still a secret. I haven't found a single picture that's been published—not even the one Jobe took.

Alexander gently pushes me behind a nearby crowd of people.

"Did you see that?" he whispers.

"I did. What do we do?" I ask.

"I'm not sure. Did you see where it came from?"

I shake my head.

"Okay. You go to the ladies restroom. Pretend you're checking your makeup. Keep your eyes open for anyone acting…strangely. Anyone watching you."

Anyone watching? I fight the heat rising to my cheeks as it occurs to me that he could very well be describing me. The person *watching* could be me, any other day, tracking a celebrity for a client. I try to swallow the lump in my throat. Is this how I make the celebrities I'm researching feel?

Of course not. I don't take pictures, and the celebrities don't even know I'm there.

I give Alexander a tight smile and head to the ladies room.

There is only one woman in the restroom. After a quick assessment, I decide I am safe; she doesn't have a camera, and her phone is nowhere in sight. She notices me watching her so I smile.

"You don't have any gum, do you?" I ask to cover my staring.

"No, sorry." She glides lipstick over her lips, smashes them together, and walks out the door.

I smooth back a few stray hairs and apply another layer of gloss over my lips. I think about wearing my hair down to confuse the alleged photographer but that would be pointless. This photographer wants a picture of me with Alexander. It doesn't matter what I look like, only that I'm standing next to him.

I turn around and lean on the counter, waiting a few minutes before I start to head back out. The door swooshes open, and two young women in their early twenties walk in. They don't seem to notice or care that I'm standing there.

"Did you see him? I can't believe Alexander Young is here," the short one with perfect blond hair and big boobs says.

"He is so handsome. And those arms? I wouldn't mind them holding me all night long," the tall, less attractive one with several piercings and tattoos says.

"Let's try to talk to him," the blond says.

"Definitely. You never know where it can lead." As she says this, her eyebrows lift twice and they both start giggling.

I can't listen. It's one thing to *think* all women want to sleep with my boyfriend, but to actually *hear* them plot and plan it is just too much. I clear my throat and turn to the mirror to check how I look, although this time I'm not pretending. I can't help but compare myself to these two women who seem to think they have a chance with Alexander. The short one has some attractive qualities, nevertheless, there is something about them, which I can't quite put my finger on, that tells me they wouldn't have a chance with Alexander, even if I wasn't in the picture.

"What?" the pierced one says to me. "You'd try too, if there was a chance he'd go for you." She eyes me from head to toe and then turns to the blond and rolls her eyes. The blond doesn't seem to notice as she's too busy primping herself in the mirror.

I take this as my cue to go to the bar and claim my boyfriend... without the photographer seeing.

I step out of the bathroom, half-expecting a flash to go off as I do. But I'm safe as long as I'm not standing next to Alexander. I look around for him. There is a crowd of people at the bar, though none of them seem to be him. I look over at the lanes; all I see are those who took the lane we should be bowling in right now. I walk out toward the back of the room, hoping to find him along the way.

I take about five steps when I feel someone grab my arm and pull me into a dark corner. *Please, let this be Alexander.* As my eyes focus in the darkness, I see him there, looking at me, a Spare Room baseball cap on.

"What is going on?" I ask.

"I found him. The photographer," he whispers. "He's on the other side of that crowd over there, leaning on the bar. See him? He's alone, wearing khaki pants and a Hawaiian shirt. I don't think he knows where we are."

He is staring intently at this man. The innocent-looking man at the bar. The one who could ruin my career and could.... what? Why is Alexander so scared of having us photographed together? Especially after those photos Jobe Graff took?

"Here's the plan, I'll go first. You follow a minute or so after me. We'll meet at the elevator. Once the doors close, we can talk about how to get to the car."

I open my mouth to respond, but before I get the chance to say anything, he is gone. I watch him as he casually walks toward the front door. He looks calm, as though he wasn't just hiding in a dark corner, planning an escape. A small group of guys watch him and nod their heads in greeting as he walks by. Alexander nods back. I wonder what they'll tell their friends tomorrow—"Alexander Young said hi to me"?

If they had come to my office, they would have gotten more than just a nod.

What?! I stop myself from slipping into Olivia work mode. Maybe this photographer has me rattled too.

Alexander is ten feet from the door when *they* step in front of him, stopping him dead in his tracks. The Bathroom Girls. The ones I would normally refer to as Hotel Girls. The blond is batting her eyelashes at him, sticking her boobs out even farther and saying something. I can only imagine what. He smiles at her, and my heart sinks. Then he nods and tries to walk past her, headed for the exit.

That's when pierced girl steps in. One hand is on her hip, the other is reaching for Alexander, about to rub his arm. *My* his arm. Unable to watch this, I start walking toward the exit, following Alexander's path. The same guys who nodded at him smile at me when I walk by. I ignore them.

My heart is pounding faster and faster as I approach the intruding duo. I smile and greet them with a simple, "Ladies." I squeeze my way between Alexander and the pierced girl, knocking her hand off of his arm and grabbing his hand as I do.

"Ready to go, babe?" I ask Alexander and, without waiting for him to respond, I walk out the door, him willingly following along.

I want to turn back. I really want to turn back. What I would give to see the faces of those girls as I take "their" man, the same man they thought I didn't have a chance with. Instead, I let go of his hand when we reach the hallway and pretend not to know him until we are alone in the elevator and the doors have safely closed behind us. Then I turn to him, and as I'm about to kiss him, he grabs me. One warm hand behind my neck, the other holding my hip, threatening to slip lower, and he kisses me. One of those kisses I know I'll never forget. The kind with fireworks going off outside and the world actually stopping. As the elevator starts to slow and he pulls away, I am tempted to hit the "stop" button. But a niggling reminder of why we're hiding in this elevator to begin with brings me back to the present.

"Go through the lobby and out to the parking lot. I'll meet you at the car," he whispers just as the elevator dings and the doors start to open. Then he walks out as if nothing has happened, as if he doesn't know me. As if he was some normal guy using the elevator to get to another floor.

I walk out through the lobby, still trying to compose myself after the kiss of a lifetime.

Alexander is waiting for me at the car. He is standing by the driver's side, though my door is open. We get in without talking, and he drives us out of the parking lot, looking in the rearview mirror several times. I assume it's to make sure we aren't being followed. We drive for a few minutes before either of us says anything.

"So—" I start. "You sure didn't want that paparazzi to get any pictures of you…of us."

"Yeah, I know. It's not how we planned for our night to go." He pauses. "It's kind of hard to explain."

I wonder for the first time if maybe there is something Alexander is hiding from me. Even though I don't have any right to be mad when it comes to this topic, I can't help but feel a little… something. Betrayed, maybe?

"Try me," I encourage him.

I can tell he is thinking of what to say and how to say it by the way he's furrowing his brow. That's his thinking face. I know what I want to ask, afraid of what the answer might be, but I have to know. I take a deep breath.

"Is it me?" I ask. "Do you not want to be seen with me?" I hold my breath as I wait for him to answer.

He closes his eyes briefly and then pulls over to the side of the street. He turns to me. "No." he says sternly. "Is that what you were thinking all this time?" He dips his head and rests it between his thumb and fingers.

I sit silently, not really sure if he wants me to answer. He shifts the car into park and puts his hand on mine.

"It is absolutely not you. The paparazzi, the tabloids, people trying to make money off of someone else's fame—they're something I try to avoid altogether. Nothing good comes from them. Normally I just ignore them. I don't live a flashy enough life for them to write about me. But tonight, with you…" he pauses, rubbing his brow again, "I just don't want us to be something they can write about. I don't want you to have to deal with all the stuff that I deal with because I'm in this line of work."

I hear everything he is saying. It is so incredibly sweet, though all I'm thinking is that he tries to avoid *me*. Or at least people like me, people who make money off of someone else's fame. Part of me thinks I need to tell him what I do right now so he knows that's not why I do what I do. Another part of me wants to find a way to hide my business from him forever, to find a way to have him never intersect with that part of me.

Every part of me wants to grab and kiss him.

"Okay," I say, because what else can I say?

He leans in and kisses me, his hand brushing my hair off my face. I can hear the fireworks begin to go off. When he pulls away, I find the courage to say what's been on my mind all night.

"You were okay with Jobe Graff photographing us." I'm not sure how to word my question so I hope he understands what I'm saying.

"Jobe Graff is different. He works with us, not against us. He knows how the game is played."

I look at him, my lips twisted, not sure I'm following.

"Jobe would never release those photos to the press without asking me first. He knows that pictures like that…they're for us."

Now I understand. He never had any intention of pictures of us being released. He didn't take me to the premiere to share me with *the* world; he took me to the premiere for me to share *his* world. As all this starts to make sense, I realize that I'm not the only one who is living in two worlds.

Alexander, and most likely all the celebrities I arrange meetings with, live two separate lives. The normal life where they do things like shop, run errands, and go on dates, and the celebrity life where they greet fans, film movies, and get photographed by the paparazzi.

My business, the one I am so passionate about and so fiercely defend as an ethical practice, makes those two worlds drastically collide, the same two worlds that Alexander tries so desperately to keep separate.

He leans in and kisses my cheek. "Should we head back to my place?" he asks.

I nod, too afraid that if I try to speak, my mind will betray my heart.

CHAPTER
25

I PULL MY CAR INTO THE parking lot and take my usual spot, right in front of Maurice's newsstand. I'm due to pick up my regular stack of tabloids. I tap my fingers on the steering wheel, stalling for time. What if the photo is published? The one both Alexander and I are so afraid exists.

My muscles relax slightly. Maybe it won't be there. Maybe the lighting was awful. Or maybe it turned out too blurry to use. I glance in the mirror visor and then take a deep breath, hoping it will erase the worry lines that seem lately to be permanently etched into my brow.

As the doorbell jingles, Maurice turns and smiles. "Hey! How's my favorite tabloid reader? I've got your regulars right over here." He slowly slides off his stool and shuffles to a back room.

I start flipping through some of the newer, less reliable tabloids, to see if there is any information that might be useful. Or any damning evidence. "Jennifer Aniston Gives Birth to Two-Headed Alien!" No. "Tom and Girlfriend Vacation on the Sunken Titanic!" Boring. "Adam Levine Saves 500 Kids from Fire in South America." Useless.

"There must be some good info in this one." He smiles his old-man smile as he holds up a trembling issue of *Tell Me* and waves it in the air. "They're selling like hotcakes. I almost had to pry this copy out of a young lady's hand." He winks.

"You always take good care of me." I smile at him.

"And," he lowers his voice and motions his wrinkled hand for me to come closer, even though we are the only ones in the store, "I've got something good for you. Rumor has it there's proof that Alexander Young's got a new girlfriend. And Sue at the juice shop down the street said he was in Saturday morning for a protein shake, and he was glowing." He points at a picture of Alexander on the cover of a magazine.

I freeze, trying to process two things at once. Proof that Alexander has a girlfriend. What kind of proof? And Alexander was glowing? My heart warms at the thought that I make him glow. I try to play it cool.

"Really? Very interesting."

"That's what Sue says." He shrugs. Maurice loves having important information.

"Good to know. Keep me posted if he comes back." I hand him the money I owe and head out.

As I slide in my car, I toss the stack of tabloids onto the passenger seat. I fight the urge to frantically scramble through them, searching for any tiny photo. I should wait—the privacy of my own office would be a much better place to absorb this kind of blow. I turn on my favorite jazz radio station and focus on the strumming of the bass and the flowing notes of the sax. Once my hands are no longer itching to leave the steering wheel, I put the car in drive and head to the office.

Twenty minutes later, I find myself sitting at my desk in a blissful state of denial. There are no tabloids. There are no secrets. I have nothing to be afraid of. Then my carefree ignorance comes slamming to a halt when half the stack of tabloids slides to the floor. Sitting on the top of what's left of the stack is the front page of *Tell Me*, and staring right at me is Alexander's gorgeous face.

The photo. The secret.

I try to distract myself, this time by looking at the calendar on the wall and the upcoming client meetings I have scheduled. When looking at all the initials scrawled on dates, I can't help but think that I should add Alexander's initials. Not to arrange a meeting but to give myself a deadline to tell him the truth.

I reach for the cappuccino I got on my way from Maurice's and realize it's nearly gone. I need more caffeine. I can barely keep my eyes open after tossing and turning most of the night. My mind kept going back and forth between what would happen if the picture was published and telling Alexander the truth. I used to think he would understand, but now, after the paparazzi incident, I'm not so sure.

I look back at the stack of fresh tabloids on my desk. I re-stack them and square in front of me is the one with Alexander's face and the headline that reads, "Breaking News!" Strumming my fingers, I try to come up with a reason why looking through this magazine is a bad idea. I can come up with a dozen. And I can come up with two dozen as to why I *have* to look.

Bravely, I turn the page to the article, and there they are. The words that I've been dreading to read. "Alexander Young's Girlfriend Revealed." I feel my heart sink just a tiny bit...until I see the actual picture.

It's not me. IT'S NOT ME!

I look closer to see who this girl is that everyone thinks is his girlfriend. *Should I be worried?*

I see piercings. Lots of them. And tattoos.

I hear a loud gasp come from my mouth. It's one of the Bathroom Girls. Not even the pretty one with big boobs. But how? I must've been so caught up in proving to them that I am good enough for

Alexander that I didn't notice the flash go off. And the suspected paparazzi? Alexander must have been wrong. The only person standing by the front door was the lady with the book, the one who works there.

I can't help but laugh. If this is who the world thinks is Alexander's girlfriend, then by all means, let them. In fact, this could actually help me. If the tabloids are looking for a pierced, tattooed girl, then no one will think anything of it when he's out with me.

I hop off my chair and do a little dance, half raise-the-roof, half hip-shaking. I need to call Alexander and give him the good news. I dial his number and wait.

"Hey, Liv," his sweet, sexy voice says. I still can't get over that voice. My heart skips just a little every time I hear it.

"Hey. I have some good news."

"What's that?" he asks. I can hear him closing a door and the background noise fades.

"Well...I was just going through this tabloid, and I came across a picture of you and your girlfriend."

"This is the good news? And why were you reading the tabloids?"

"It's not me," I interrupt, ignoring the second part of his question.

"Huh?"

"The picture. It's not me." I clarify.

"Then who is it?"

"Well, it looks like a picture was snapped of you with the girls who approached you just as we were leaving. Specifically, the one with piercings and tattoos." I wait to hear his response.

After a few moments pass, he starts to chuckle. "Not even the better-looking one?"

"Not even the better-looking one," I say.

"That's great. Now the paparazzi will be looking for me and someone with piercings and tattoos. I guess you're a little too average for them."

"I guess so." Coming from anyone but Alexander, I would have been insulted. But I know he means it in a good way, in the way I try to get my clients to be average.

"So why are you reading the tabloids? I didn't know you read them," he asks again.

I can't believe this slipped past me. I've been so careful to keep my work under wraps and I make this stupid slip.

"Olivia?" he asks.

I have to think of something quick. "I...I haven't been sleeping well." This is true. "I keep thinking about what could happen if our picture is in a tabloid." Also true. "So I've been checking for our picture." This last part is less true.

"I didn't mean to worry you," he says. "All this tabloid stuff is my job, not yours. I don't want you to worry about it. Let me do that."

How can I possibly respond to this? It seems I just keep digging myself deeper and deeper into this hole. The tabloid stuff IS my job. More than he could ever understand. Which brings to my attention, yet again, how wrong the tabloids can be. I grasp for some way to answer him.

"Okay?" he asks.

"Okay," I respond, unable to think of anything else.

"But since we do seem to be off the hook, at least this time, how about we go out and celebrate? I have a few things to wrap up here and then I can swing by your place and pick you up."

I wish I could forget everything and run away with Alexander. But I have a meeting scheduled with Becky.

"Can we meet up a little later? I should be done around four. How about we meet at La Boheme?"

"Sure, sounds perfect," he says.

As we hang up, I notice it's later than I thought. Becky is due to be here in just a few minutes, and I need to prepare for the meeting. I grab the stack of tabloids and pile them into a cabinet, out of sight. I toss my empty coffee cup into the trash and realize that, again, I've managed to spill on my shirt. I get a scarf out of a drawer and head to the bathroom to straighten up.

Just as I am finishing, I hear a knock on the door. I unlock the file drawer in my desk, fling it open, and recklessly yank on Becky's file, sending a few other files into chaos. As I stand up, I swiftly kick the drawer to shut it and race to the door to let her in.

Looking at Becky sitting in that big puffy chair with one leg draped over the arm and her mind buried in a *National Geographic* magazine, you'd never guess that she was about to meet her favorite celebrity. I grab just the basics: breath mints, floss, clothing tape, deodorant, a comb, and hairspray. I tuck everything neatly in my bag and take a moment to observe Becky. She seems calm. Too calm.

"Becky? Are you ready?"

"What?" For a brief moment she looks at me as though she's not sure where she is or why she's there. Then I see the reality set in as she starts to quickly bounce her dangling leg. "Of course! I was just reading this fascinating article about elephants and their relationships with—"

She recognizes the baffled look on my face.

"I was keeping my mind busy so that I wouldn't get too nervous. It's so much easier to not think about how I'll soon be sitting in the same room as Robert Collins and all the different ways this can turn out. I know I'm ready. I've practiced every scenario we've anticipated."

"You're going to do great. I've never worked with someone as well prepared as you. Let's go over the scenarios again. If he says he *has to have* his manicurist—"

"Then I say she is my manicurist as well. He doesn't own her." She nods.

"If he pretends you aren't even there and simply sits in his chair," I continue.

"I walk over and sit in the manicurists seat until she comes over and helps us resolve it. I hope that doesn't happen. That one stresses me out the most."

"That is a tough one. But it still gets you talking with him. So… what if he turns and says something demeaning to you?"

"I tell him I'm sorry he feels that way, but I still need my nails done because I have an important event and stick to that story until he asks what event could possibly be more important than his television show. And I tell him it's the charity event for autism."

"Exactly. Remember, that's his soft spot. That charity event is our fallback. If all else fails, find a way to bring it up. He is on the charity's board and is very involved in the organization. He is cohosting the event this year. He doesn't need to know you're not really going."

"I'm ready. Let's do this." She bounces to her feet and grabs her bag.

I grab my purse and we head out the door.

I arrive at the salon a few minutes before Becky, to check in. Once the desk has my name, I take a seat and disappear behind a magazine. I peep my eyes over the top of my reading material and survey the situation. There are two people getting their nails done and one woman waiting for her nails to dry. The much-coveted manicurist is cleaning up her station. In fact, she seems to be paying extra attention to detail and making sure things are just where they should be. At exactly 4:28, Becky waltzes in. She is truly adorable today in her blue skinny jeans, white blouse, and black heels. The lavender scarf tied at the front gives her a mature look, fitting to her personality. She approaches the front desk and waits for the receptionist to finish her call.

The receptionist knows Becky by now and greets her by name. "Hi, Becky. Let's see." She glances down at her book. "Today we have you with Lilly."

Becky feigns confusion. "Oh, but I always use Marina."

The door jingles softly and Robert Collins walks in. He approaches and nods at the receptionist.

"Can you switch me to Marina?" Becky continues.

The receptionist lowers her voice. "I'm sorry, Becky. Marina is already booked at this time. Lilly is wonderful and will do just as good of a job."

"But I have an important event coming up," Becky insists. "I would really like Marina to do my nails."

The receptionist quickly glances to Robert Collins and back at Becky. "I'm sorry, it's just not possible today."

Robert sees the receptionist looking between him and Becky and senses the distress in her expression. "Is there a problem?"

"No, Mr. Collins, not at all," she assures him.

"Then why can't I see Marina today?" Becky says louder this time.

Before the receptionist can respond, Robert interrupts. "Is that the problem? She wants to see Marina today?"

Becky sees the opportunity and goes for it. "Yes. I always see Marina, and I have an important event this weekend. But for some reason, they won't let me see her today."

Robert takes a moment. I cringe in my seat, not knowing what to expect. *Please don't unleash a fury of swear words onto innocent Becky. Please, please, please.* He looks her over from head to toe and then turns back to Amy. "She can have Marina today. Who else do you have for me?"

I see that Becky is ready to attack, just as we had planned. It takes her a moment to take in what has just happened. She recuperates and smiles at Robert. "Thank you. That is very nice of you." He doesn't hear the last part she says. He doesn't even acknowledge her. He just follows the receptionist to his chair.

When he is settled in, the receptionist comes back to take me to my chair, then Becky to hers.

After our hands are massaged and nails are painted and pretty, we meet outside the salon. I take Becky for coffee to the café down the street to discuss what happened. Neither of us really know what to make of the situation. In all the scenarios we had come up with, not one of them included Robert being polite. I am happy that Becky got to see a polite side of Robert, but I feel like I let her down. I should've anticipated this as a possibility, no matter how unlikely it was. She did *sort of* get a meeting with him. But it was clearly not what either of us was expecting.

Becky taps her fingers on the table as she stares into her coffee. I'm trying hard not to bite my lip as I scan her face for some hint as to what she's thinking. "Are you okay? How do you feel about what happened?"

"I don't know. I mean, I'm a little bit disappointed that I didn't really get to *talk* to him. But he was *polite* to me. He's not polite to anyone." She looks at me with a big smile. Suddenly she isn't looking at me but behind me.

"Have fun at your event this weekend," a deep voice says.

"Thanks," Becky replies.

I turn just in time to see Robert Collins looking down at Becky and the small pin on her blouse. I hadn't noticed it before; now I see that it has the Autism Research Institute emblem on it. I catch Becky's eye, and lift my eyebrows to her pin. Once Robert is gone she says, "I got it when I donated to the charity a few weeks ago. I figured it couldn't hurt to wear it."

Just like that, the meeting is a success.

CHAPTER
26

WITH ANOTHER SUCCESSFUL CLIENT -meeting under my belt, I find it hard not to skip as I make my way down the hall toward my office. I play what happened over in my head and think about how I can apply the same method in the future. Then my mind starts to wander to my evening plans with Alexander. I have just enough time to drop my things off in the office and head over to La Boheme.

As I approach my office door, I stop still. The door is open a crack. My heart starts to pound. Who could be in my office? Thoughts flash through my mind of what would happen if all my files and notes get into the wrong hands. I listen for any sound that might be coming from the other side of the door. Nothing.

Slowly, I put my trembling hand on the knob and very cautiously nudge open the door. I peek inside and everything looks normal. The big fluffy chair is empty; there aren't papers on the floor. I start thinking that maybe, just maybe, I accidentally left the door open in my rush to get to the meeting this morning. Gaining more confidence, I push the door wide open and my heart drops into my stomach. What I see is much, much worse than anything I possibly could have imagined.

Sitting at my desk amid piles of shuffled-through files is Alexander.

Unsure of what to say, I stand there staring at him, his head resting heavily in his hands, his elbows weighing on the edge of the desk.

"Alexander," I start, but he doesn't look at me.

I hear a deep sigh. I'm not sure if it comes from him or me. One of his hands drops to the desk as he starts to speak.

"What is all this, Olivia?" His voice is different. It sounds… injured.

"It's—" I try to think about how I can explain this, how to tell him what it is without saying what it means. "It's my work."

"Your work?" He says it as though he doesn't want to believe what he's hearing. He looks at me, and I can see his eyes are red. How long has he been here, going through my files?

"Yes. I—" Before I can start he interrupts.

"Your work?" he says louder. He holds up the folder with his name on the tab. With the post-it on the front that clearly says, "Clara-Alexander: Plan for next meeting" with all the tabloid articles and Clara's handwritten notes. "What exactly *is* your work? Because it looks to me like you get paid to help people stalk celebrities."

I have to say something, but all those times I'd rehearsed how I was going to tell him, now that I have to say something, nothing comes out. The arguments that I had come up with that explained what I do seemed so *logical*, though what I'm feeling right now is *not*.

"It's not like that," I manage to mumble.

"Then what?" he demands, shaking his head. "Tell me what it is like. Tell me, because I don't understand. I thought we were—"

"We are. I want to explain." I step closer and close the door behind me, but I can't find the right words. "I arrange meetings for people. I'm good at it, so I thought I'd help people meet their favorite celebrities in normal ways, like at the post office or—"

"Or at the grocery store?" he asks.

"Yes!" I instinctively respond, thinking that maybe he's starting to understand. But then *I* understand what he's implying, and it's too late. "I mean no—"

"So that's all I am. Just a meeting at the grocery store that you were preparing for—" He looks down at the file in front of him. "For Clara."

"No," I cry. "No, you weren't. Our meeting was an accident."

"Yeah, you can say that again."

"Alexander," I plead, "you have nothing to do with my work. Someone asked for you *once*, and I purposely arranged it so that you wouldn't be there."

"I saw." He runs his hand through his hair. "You used what I told you privately as my *girlfriend*, in confidence, to arrange a meeting at the car wash."

I have never heard him call me his "girlfriend."

"No, I told her to go when you were with me." *I chose you!* I want to scream. "I wasn't using you. In fact, dating you was a risk because if my clients found out—"

"Olivia," he says, his voice flat, "I just wanted to be with you. That's it. Nothing else."

"This isn't what you think," I insist.

"I knew from the moment I knocked you off your feet that I wanted to be with you." He looks at me, his eyebrows arched. His voice softens. "But I guess *you* knew it before that."

He gets up and walks out.

On my desk, sitting on top of all the rifled through files, is a picture. The picture Jobe took of us kissing on the night of Alexander's premiere.

I fall to the floor and start to cry.

CHAPTER
27

MARIA SHOWS UP ON MY front door with two bottles of wine and a large tub of rocky road. My eyes are so puffy from crying that I can barely see her through the peephole.

"Aw, sweetie!" she coos as she puts the medicinal ice cream on the nearest table and wraps her arms around me. "Have you stopped crying even for a second?"

I open my mouth to respond, and nothing comes out but a sob. I blow my nose and throw the tissue on the pile on the floor. Maria pulls back from me and looks around.

"We have got to clean this up, sweetie," she whispers as she starts to scoop the tissues, empty soda cans, and torn tabloids into the trash.

"I should've told him," I cry. "I should've told him that night. Instead of getting even more attached, I should've told him the truth." I keep replaying that evening in my head, when we were at his house and he opened up to me. I should have told him what I do, instead of being seduced by those luring eyes and sexy arms.

I keep wondering how things would have turned out differently if only I had been the one to tell him, if only I had been able to put my own spin on it so he could see that what I do isn't so bad.

"He said he thought I met him on purpose." I cough and take a deep breath. "He thinks it was all part of a big, crazy plan."

Maria nods and hands me another tissue. I wipe my eyes.

"How can he believe that? I thought he knew me."

"He does know you," she assures me. "Maybe he just needs some time."

"He's had time," I sigh. "It's been two days! He's not coming back. I just need to face it. We're done, and I...I will be alone and sad and *average* forever."

A muffled sound comes from the sofa. We hear it again. Suddenly I realize it's my phone. I dive onto the cushions, tossing the pillows haphazardly, trying to find it before it stops ringing. Maybe it's him! Maybe he's calling to say he's overreacted!

I find the phone as it lets out its third ring. Without even glancing at who it is, afraid I will miss the call if I do, I hit the answer button without hesitation.

"Hello?" I say all too quickly and eagerly.

"Hi," a familiar male voice quips back. "Are you okay?"

It's Charlie. I hand the phone to Maria and throw my face into one of the pillows to silence my sobs. I can hear her talking to him in bits and pieces. First she says, "She's pretty messed up about it," then she adds, "I don't think you should," and finally she ends with, "No, I really don't think she's up for that."

I'm guessing Charlie told Preston about the ugly incident. They're probably gloating over the fact that they were right and I was wrong, that the relationship was doomed from the start, that I really am just a "normal, average" girl and not in the good, useful way my clients want to be. But in the not-good-enough-for-Alexander way.

Once I hear Maria rummaging around in one of my kitchen drawers, I know it's safe so I peek out. She meets me on the sofa with two spoons and two glasses of wine. She gives me a half-hearted smile as she grabs the tub and hands me a spoon. I take a gulp of wine and let out a hollow sigh.

"It tastes just like the wine Alexander and I had on our first date," I lament.

"Of course it does," she sympathizes. "It always does."

CHAPTER
28

A WEEK LATER, I'M SITTING IN my office, painting my toenails. I finish up the small toe and wipe a smudge of the dark blue polish off with my finger. Leaning back in my chair, I shuffle through the magazines on my desk, *Self, Shape, National Geographic* and settle on the *Redbook* at the bottom of the stack, even though I've read it front to back at least a dozen times. My phone chirps. I don't even glance at who's calling and instead let it go directly to voicemail. I notice it's one o'clock and vaguely recall that I haven't eaten yet today so I swing my chair around to grab a soda from the minifridge. It's empty.

I fight back the urge to burst into tears. Over soda.

Then I wonder if this is what life will be from now on. Crying over the simplest of things for no reason at all. My phone beeps that I have a voicemail. I hit the Ignore button and send it to phone purgatory where it will wait with the other twenty-three messages.

Three knocks rattle my door. I know I don't have appointments today, as I haven't taken or made any calls all week. Maybe it's a solicitor who snuck into the building. I ignore it, hoping who ever it is will go away, a strategy I've been employing a lot lately.

The knocking persists, and I think about faking an accent and saying I don't speak English. Or climbing out the window. There's always a trellis by the second-story window in the movies, right? Then I remember, lately, my life is as far from a movie as possible. The knocks continue.

"Olivia, are you there?" a deep familiar voice asks. "Maria said you've returned to work."

I know the voice. It's Charlie.

"Please, Olivia?" he says. "I know you're there. Your car's outside, and I can see the light on under the door. You can't hide from the world forever."

Can't I? Or at least until the swelling of my eyes from all the crying goes away. Although for that to happen, I suppose I'll have to stop crying. I walk to the door and lean my head against it, thinking about letting him in.

I hear him mumble something that ends with "idiot" and spontaneously feel a fire burn inside me. Did he just call me an idiot? I swing open the door.

"What did you just say?" I huff.

He looks at me, his eyebrows furled, red rising to his cheeks. "He's an idiot, I said. For breaking up with you."

"Come on. We both know how much you and Preston disapprove of my choices. I'm sure you're both thrilled to pieces." I start to close the door. Charlie puts his hand out to stop me.

"That was Preston," he starts. "And only because he doesn't want you to get hurt. He worries about you. And I truly think Alexander's an idiot."

"Really?" I ask, fully expecting him to lay it on me that I should've seen it coming.

"Yeah," he softens, "I really think so."

I walk back to my desk and motion for him to follow. I see him looking around my office and realize he's never been here before. The space isn't exactly in its welcoming-new-guests state.

"This is—" he starts, but I interrupt him.

"A mess, I know." I sigh. "But there's not much point in cleaning it up now. Not until I figure out what's next."

"What do you mean? Are you planning to close your business? Because of Alexander?"

"I don't know," I say. "It just doesn't seem ethical anymore."

I'm not quite sure how to tell him that everything Preston said was right. Ever since Alexander ended things, I've had a lot of time to think. Once Alexander and I became involved, the world of celebrities seemed all too real. I *was* doing exactly what Alexander accused me of. I *was* getting paid to help people stalk celebrities.

How would I have felt if there had been someone watching Alexander that day we met at the grocery store? What would her notes have said? "Bumps into women and then helps them up. Follows to register." Or that day in the parking lot before we went for our first dinner? "Pays for other people's parking meters." Or the time at the observatory? "Talks with fans and doesn't mind being interrupted. Not dating anyone as there is no physical contact with the woman he was with."

All these moments of people's lives, innuendos that mostly mean nothing, that I turned into proof that celebrities enjoy contact with *normal* people, strangers. Of course they do! They're human! But for me to take sincere experiences and hijack them, for money no less, so that my clients can have their moment, much like with a zoo animal, just isn't right. In fact, it seems inhuman. And this is what Preston had been saying all along.

But I don't know how to express this to Charlie. Not because I'm afraid he'll tell Preston, but because I don't want to look like a fool or a failure in front of him. Maria is right, Charlie has always believed in me and my business. It was when this whole Alexander situation started that he began to act...funny.

"You can't quit now, Liv," he offers again. "You've worked so hard to get where you are. You have so many clients who count on you to help make their dreams come true."

"But their dreams aren't the only ones that count, right?" I suggest. "What about the celebrity who dreams of going to the store and not being bothered. Or maybe the girlfriend who doesn't want to share her celebrity boyfriend with a fan?"

"Being famous comes with some downsides. And belonging to the public is one of them. Believe me, it may be a pain sometimes, but once they realize that those people coming up to them when they're on dates or at the grocery store are the same ones who buy tickets to their movies or concerts, they find a way to live with it if not enjoy it."

This reminds me of something Alexander had said on a date once—how he likes to keep his fans happy. It was what convinced me he'd understand when I had gotten around to telling him what I do, or did, for a living. Clearly, I had read him wrong.

And then I start to wonder something, something, for once, that has nothing to do with Alexander. Why is Charlie here? Why is he always so willing to help me? Like that time he showed up with Tommy's after the Eva incident. Or how I heard him swearing at Preston that night after we got into a fight. And he's always more than willing to give me information about celebrities. What was it Maria had said about him going out of his way to see me?

I wonder if there's something I've been missing all along.

"Why are you here, Charlie?" I ask pointedly. "Preston didn't send you, did he?"

He seems caught off guard and sits up in the big puffy chair, that doesn't look quite so big with him sitting in it. He takes a moment to gather what he's going to say. "I want to make sure you're okay," he starts. "Maria was worried, and you haven't returned my calls. So I thought I'd come down and make sure—"

I raise my eyebrows, curious as to what he's going to say.

"I care about you, Olivia. A lot," he hesitates. "I want to take care of you. Maybe it's because I've known you for so long, or maybe it's more. But I want to be there for you."

I push a strand of hair behind my ear, thinking about how I look for the first time in days. Sweatpants and an old UCLA shirt. Did I even brush my hair this morning? I hear what Charlie is saying, and as much as I could enjoy every word of it and read all sorts of wonderful things into it, I don't. All I can think about is Alexander.

"At least let me take you to lunch. You look like you haven't eaten much lately."

I'm ready to say no when I consider that I should probably eat. And the box of cereal at home doesn't sound very appetizing.

That night as I lay in bed, my mind starts wandering back to Alexander. I wonder if he's cuddled up on his sofa in those flannel pants he likes so much. Or maybe he's out on the town, wearing that purple shirt that makes his eyes so green, drinking a Scotch, no ice.

The clock flashes 10:07. We were usually talking at this time if he was out of town working or we were together if he wasn't. I start wondering if he misses me as much as I miss him. He had become such a normal part of my life. My only comfort is in knowing that he must at least feel like something is missing, that there is time he has to fill during his day to make up for when we were together. Even if he doesn't want to remember that he spent that time with me.

To help me fall asleep I replay one of the many days Alexander and I hung out, a coping mechanism I've used a lot in the past week to help me get through. The way he held my hand and caressed my thumb or brushed the hair from my cheek...

CHAPTER

29

AT SEVEN A.M. SHARP, MY doorbell rings. I finish pulling my hair into a casual bun on the top of my head and smush my lips together to help spread the lip gloss, my only attempt to look decent. I grab some sunscreen, toss it into my bag as I sling it over my shoulder, and open the door. Charlie greets me with his normal huge smile.

Yesterday he talked me into going for a hike in the Santa Monica Mountains. I'm not really sure of Charlie's intentions. For right now, though, I don't really care what they are. Having someone to hang around with who reminds me nothing of Alexander is a nice distraction.

Plus, Charlie is lots of fun, and I'd probably think those curly blond locks and bright blue eyes were attractive if I hadn't known him since I was in diapers.

The clear sky and bright sun lift my spirits as we pull in to the dirt parking lot and get out of the car. Charlie grabs two waters from his trunk and walks over to my door. I'm tightening my hiking boots when I realize my socks don't match. Oh well. I shuffle through my bag to see what essentials I need to bring with me, and my sunscreen falls out. Charlie picks it up.

"Good idea," he says. "I forgot to bring mine."

I stand up as he squirts some into his hands and starts slathering it over his arms and face.

"Looks like I got too much," he says. "Here, let me get your shoulders."

His warm hands feel nice on my skin. I close my eyes, and before I know it, my heart has taken over, and I am imagining it is Alexander rubbing in lotion, not Charlie. When he goes to get more lotion, I stop him.

"It's okay," I say, my voice a little too high. "I'll do the rest."

We start up the trail. As fresh air fills my lungs and my heart rate starts increasing, I find I'm happy here. We pass several hikers, greeting them as we make room for each other on the often narrow path.

Charlie seems to be avoiding the topic of Alexander. Instead, we make small talk about work and reminisce over the trouble he and Preston used to get into and how Maria and I couldn't wait to tell on them. He is in the middle of rehashing the time that Preston and he got caught sneaking out to see some sci-fi movie on the night of its release when a pair of hikers approach, nodding to me and addressing Charlie.

"Hey, man," the guy in sunglasses and a hat says. His voice is familiar.

"What's up?" Charlie says back. "Good to see you. How're the wife and baby?"

"They're great. I can't believe how much he's grown in just a few weeks," he responds. His voice is *very* familiar.

"This is my friend, Olivia," Charlie puts his hand to my back as he introduces me.

"Hi, Olivia, nice to meet you," the *incredibly* familiar voice says.

And suddenly it hits me why the voice is so familiar. It's the same voice I've dreamed about my entire life. The same voice that sang me to sleep every night of my teenage life. The very same voice that played nonstop on my radio for years (and still occasionally does, if I'm being honest).

Brad Griffin is standing not two feet away from me, hand extended, waiting for me to take it. How did I not see it was him? It is so obvious now—those gorgeous blue eyes hiding behind his glasses, the slight Boston accent seeping through his words.

Oh my goodness. I must respond. I open my mouth and nothing comes out. So I extend my arm to shake his hand but miss, and instead we hit thumbs. I try to speak again.

"Hi," I barely mumble, moving my hand to where it belongs. "It's nice to good, I mean—"

Charlie looks at me. I look back at him, my eyes wide, my free hand just barely, visibly shaking. At first he looks confused. Then I watch as he starts to smile, and his eyes grow just slightly larger as well.

"Sorry, we've been hiking for a while," Charlie interrupts. "I think she's dehydrated from the heat. Here, Olivia, have some water." He grabs a bottle out of his backpack and hands it to me. Then he turns back to Brad and changes the subject, giving me the few precious moments needed to get a grip.

Deep breaths. I keep telling myself, *remember, he's just like you.* Damn it! I learned affirmations don't work when I tried using them on my first date with Alexander! Oh, Alexander. I feel the sadness grabbing onto my heart and starting to squeeze. Stop! Brad Griffin is RIGHT IN FRONT OF YOU, and you're brooding over Alexander? SNAP OUT OF IT!

And just like that...

"I'm sorry. I think I've recovered. I wasn't expecting it to be so hot today." I brush my hair behind my ear. "Congratulations on your new baby. How old is he?"

We spend the next five minutes making small talk, with me (hopefully) redeeming myself, and Charlie mostly watching. When it's time to continue on our separate ways, I gracefully extend my hand, my palm landing squarely in his, and I say, "It was really nice to meet you."

"Nice meeting you too," he responds. "Don't forget to drink your water. You wouldn't want to make poor Charlie carry you home."

Brad Griffin turns the corner, and Charlie heads up the path while I lag behind.

"I can't believe I forgot what a fan you are of Brad Griffin. He just joined our publicity agency, and it hadn't occurred to me to tell you until you were standing here, stumbling like a teenage boy on his first date." He starts laughing and then turns when he realizes I'm not following him. "Liv? What's the matter?"

I can hardly bring myself to say it. "I think—"

"What? What is it?"

"I think he called me fat!"

"Who called you fat?"

"Brad Griffin," I huff. "Brad Griffin just called me fat! He said, 'You wouldn't want to make poor Charlie carry you home.' Why else would he say that?"

"I don't think that's what he meant."

"Do you know what that means?" My heart is racing so fast I can barely speak slow enough for him to understand me. "It means that not only does he *not* think of me as a fan, but that he actually looked at my body! Brad Griffin *looked* at *my* body!"

Charlie opens his mouth, and pauses, as if unsure of what to say.

"Oh My God! Is my hair okay? Wait, I don't have any makeup on! Did I even brush my teeth this morning?" I lift my arm and sniff. "I think I put on deodorant."

Charlie shakes his head and starts laughing. "You look great. And smell great too. And if those didn't impress him, I'm sure your calm and collected personality did."

I look at him, my lips twisted, head tilted. I start walking and playfully punch his arm as I pass.

And just like that, the world starts to look brighter.

CHAPTER
30

I STARE INTO MY CLOSET, LOOKING for something to wear on my date with Charlie. *Date with Charlie.* It just sounds weird—I've never once thought about dating him. He is certainly good-looking, but I've known him since before I knew what attractive is, so it's hard to think of him as attractive.

He's always been my brother's best friend. After my parents died, he became one of my best friend's too; he is always there. I've known him even longer than I've known Maria. I clearly remember when he was seven and grounded for feeding Kool-Aid to his dog to see if it would change the color of its pee. And how he hid in his room for nearly a week when he was fifteen because his girlfriend broke up with him. And how in college, during semester breaks, he would always try to get Preston to go to parties with him and how disappointed he'd become when Preston would choose to stay home to prepare for his upcoming classes instead.

When Charlie asked if I would go on a date with him, I couldn't come up with a real reason to say no, so here I am, wondering what to wear on my date with Charlie.

I pull out a pair of dark jeans and a sexy red top and put them on the bed next to a blue dress. I reach into the bottom of my closet for a pair of shoes, when a green dress catches my eye. It's a dress I bought to go out with Alexander and only wore once. My first thought is to shove it where I'll never have to look at it again. But then I remember how delicately the straps lay across my shoulders and how the neckline falls just right and how the hem hits midthigh. Alexander had said I was "quite the sight" and threatened he'd keep me home had we not had tickets to a show.

Instead of throwing the dress to the back of the closet, I push all my thoughts of Alexander to the back of my mind. I slip the dress on and glance in the mirror, knowing that I've made the right choice.

As I'm finishing applying my makeup, I hear knocking at the door. I peek my head out of my bedroom and yell, "Come in, Charlie!"

He opens the door and smiles at me.

"Make yourself at home," I tell him. "I'll be out in a minute." Then I hop back into the bathroom to take my hair out of the bun and put on my lipstick.

When I step into the living room, Charlie stands up.

"You look amazing," he says as he walks over to give me a hug.

"Thanks," I say. I notice that he looks really good and smells really good too. He has an air of sophistication about him that I've never noticed before. Maybe it's the dark designer jeans he has on, or maybe it's the untucked, expensive button-down shirt he's wearing that make him look so…appealing. At the same time, I know there is something missing. I'm fully aware that this man in front of me is attractive and attracted to me. But *something*… that little skip of the heart when you see that special someone…is missing.

I find myself enjoying our hug as he holds on a little longer than he normally does. I've never noticed how much taller he is than me and how nicely I fit in his arms.

Still, no little skip of the heart.

He leans in and kisses me on the cheek. I freeze, not because I don't like it but because it's Charlie. Then I remember he's kissed me on the cheek several times in my life—after my first dance recital, when I graduated from high school, at my parents' funeral.

I pull away and smile at him. He smiles back.

"I guess we should get going. Our reservation is in a few minutes," he says.

"Ooooh, a reservation. Are we going somewhere fancy?" I ask.

"Well in that dress, we'd better be." He opens the door and waits for me to walk through.

Once we get outside, he puts his arm around me. He feels strong against my back, even though his hand is just barely holding my side. When we get to the car, he opens my door and waits for me to buckle up before closing it. I've always noticed how attentive Charlie is with his girlfriends; experiencing this for myself surprises me.

The first few minutes of the car ride are very quiet. While there are a million things to say to my *friend* Charlie, I'm not sure what to say to my *date* Charlie. When I think back to most of our conversations in the recent past, I realize how much we…or I, really…talked about Alexander.

Soon Charlie breaks the silence by asking if I'm still planning to give up my business.

"Well, that's a good question." I'm not sure how much I want to tell him. He is Preston's best friend, and I'm almost positive that anything I say will get back to my brother. Or will it? Does Preston even know we are on a date?

"And the answer is?" he kids me.

"I'm thinking about sticking with it. And I sort of have you to thank for that."

"Me?" He briefly glances at me, his eyebrows raised, before looking back at the road. "What did I do? I mean, I'm happy I could help but—"

"When you took me on that hike and we ran into Brad Griffin, it all came flooding back to me. I had forgotten how it feels to meet a celebrity you really admire. I mean to meet him and actually talk to him, and have him look at me like I'm the average girl; it was amazing."

"Even though he called you fat?"

I laugh. "Yes, even though he called me fat." I pause. "But really, after feeling that human connection with an idol, I can't give up my business. Everyone should know that feeling. I want to help my clients experience it."

Charlie smiles at me. "Well, I'm glad I could help."

"But," I continue, "how in the world did you NOT tell me that Brad Griffin was at your agency? That's basically the news of the century for me. How could you forget?"

"Well, you were a little…preoccupied…with a different celebrity. I wasn't sure you'd want to know."

He's right. I was very preoccupied, and maybe I wouldn't have cared *as* much. I'm really not sure how to respond. So I don't. Right then we pull up to the valet.

We are in front of Cecconi's, a restaurant that's notorious for its celebrity clientele. Also notorious for not tolerating any paparazzi or celebrity-disturbing behavior. Probably mostly for the latter reason, I haven't been able to gather much research on the place and, thus, never been here.

"What do you think?" Charlie asks, clearly proud of his choice.

"This is fantastic. I can't believe you were able to get a reservation."

He shrugs his shoulders and puts out his hand to guide me from the car. The valet whisks the car down the circular drive as we head toward the entrance. A man opens the door for us, and we are lead to the hostess, who promptly shows us our seat in the corner of the patio. Seated a few tables away is Julia Roberts. Charlie doesn't even blink. He is clearly trying to impress me and most likely pulled some strings to do it.

I open the menu and browse through the many options from red quinoa, to pumpkin tortellini, to squash blossoms with goat cheese and black truffles. Though everything looks delicious, I can't stop recalling the memory of my first dinner date with Alexander. I remember the menu, also Italian, but nothing like this one. And the crowd, everyone was just so normal, a bunch of average people sitting in a restaurant, eating. Alexander was so comfortable there. I was too. I try harder to push away any memories of Alexander. I'm here on a date with Charlie, after all.

Even though I'm beside someone I've known my entire life, I can't help but feel out of my comfort zone. Our small talk is more natural than it was in the car, but, still, there is something missing.

The waiter comes by to take our drink orders, and without me even opening my mouth, Charlie orders us a bottle of red wine.

"Cabernet Sauvignon is still your favorite, right?" Charlie asks.

"It is." I'm surprised that he knows my favorite wine. Do I know his favorite drink?

"I think I'm going to have the branzino. I've heard it's great. How about you?" he asks.

"The scallops sound perfect." I wonder what else he knows about me that I've taken for granted. Does Alexander know my favorite wine?

Stop! I need to focus on my date.

Charlie is the one who asked me out tonight, not Alexander. Charlie is the one who knows my favorite wine, not Alexander. And Charlie is clearly interested in dating me, not Alexander. From here on out, for the rest of the night, I pledge not to think of Alexander at all. I should at least give Charlie a fighting chance. Otherwise, what is the point of me being here?

The waiter returns with our bottle, opens it, and pours a small amount for Charlie to taste. Charlie takes the glass in his hand and swirls it, slowly sniffs it, and takes a sip, nodding to the waiter. The waiter then pours some into my glass and finishes pouring Charlie's.

When the waiter returns, Charlie orders for me. At first, I'm taken aback by this. The feminist in me wants to swear at Charlie and tell him to order his own food. And then I remember his parents were much older. He is the youngest of eight children, and they instilled old-fashioned, gentlemanlike behavior in all of the boys. I smile at Charlie and think that maybe I do know his favorite drink after all.

As our food arrives and I'm finishing my wine, I'm starting to get used to the idea of being on a date with Charlie. It's getting easier and easier to talk to him, and I don't really feel like I'm avoiding the topic of Alexander anymore. Rather, it simply isn't coming up. There is one topic, though, that is eating away at me a bit. Does Preston know we are on a date? How much does he know about Charlie and me? Does he approve?

"So, I'm really curious," I say.

"What? You can ask me anything," he says. He wipes his napkin across his mouth and rests his forearms on the table. "What are you curious about?"

"I was wondering what Preston thinks about…this."

"This? You mean you and me on a date." He says it so matter-of-factly, I'm wondering if that's how he mentioned it to Preston. "Hmm. The topic of you dating anyone is a tough one for him. But he seems okay with it. I mean, he is my best friend. I did kind of clear it with him before I asked you."

"Oh. That's good to know." I pause, unsure of how to ask the next part of the question. "So anything we say or—"

"Are you asking me if I kiss and tell?" I can tell by his deep laugh that he is teasing me. "Anything we say…or do…stays between us."

The waiter comes by to collect the bill, and we head to the car. I glance down at my watch, and it's almost ten o' clock. I know Charlie has an early day tomorrow. When he gets in the car, he hesitates before putting it in drive. He turns to me and smiles a half-smile and then pulls out of the valet line and onto the street.

As we drive home, Charlie tells me what it was like growing up as the youngest of eight siblings. He tells me how he barely knows his oldest sister, who went off to college when he was four years old. He tells me that since he shared a bedroom his entire life, when he rented his first apartment, he used to sleep in the living room with the TV on to make it feel like there were more people around.

Hearing all of these stories make me realize that even though I've hung around Charlie for as long as I can remember, there is a whole other side to him that I don't know. Since he was my brother's best friend, I never learned anything personal about him. I have been there for most of the major events of his life, though didn't know how he experienced them.

We pull up in front of my house, and he opens the car door for me. I feel his arm fall around my side as we walk up the stairs to my apartment.

Wait…now what? Do I invite him in? Do I hug him and say thank you and goodbye? Olivia, the friend, would probably invite him in for a drink. But if Olivia, the date, invites him in, isn't that implying something? I wish I could tell him to hold on so I can call Maria to ask her what to do.

We get to my door, and I decide the best strategy is to stall for time by not saying anything.

"I guess I should be going. I do have an early morning tomorrow." He smiles a shy smile at me. He seems to be having a hard time meeting my eyes. Maybe he is stalling too.

"Thanks for inviting me," I say as I unlock my door and push it slightly ajar.

"I had a really good time," he says as he jiggles his keys in one hand. "Would you like to go out again sometime?"

Would I? I think so. I may not be feeling butterflies, like I did with Alexander, but I am feeling *something*, aren't I? I'm not really sure. The something I'm feeling may just be that weird awkwardness that comes from dating your brother's best friend.

"Okay," I say.

Then I see it coming. I'm not sure what to do. It's as if everything moves in slow motion. I see him leaning toward me, I feel his arms slowly wrap around me, and then finally…his lips come down on mine.

What do I do? Do I kiss him back? I'm not sure I want to. But am I sure I don't want to? I don't know! And if I don't kiss him back, then what? Then we have that awkward moment where we both know things just went horribly wrong and nobody knows what to say. And I don't want them to go horribly wrong. What if I kiss him back and I like it? Or what if I kiss him back and I don't like it?

This shouldn't be so difficult. I abandon all feelings and just go with it.

His lips are surprisingly soft and confident. He pulls me a little tighter as he feels my lips respond, and then he pulls away.

When I open my eyes, I see him smiling at me.

"Good night, Olivia." He leans forward and kisses me on the cheek before walking down the stairs and into the night.

I can say for certain that I didn't dislike our kiss. In fact, I think I might have even enjoyed it. Still, there is something missing, like that little skip of the heart. I toss my purse onto my coffee table and think about calling Maria to dissect our date. But I'm not sure there's anything to dissect.

Even though I had a great time with Charlie, I still can't quite conjure up that feeling that can come so naturally. That *I belong here* feeling.

Then it occurs to me. Of course something's missing. This whole dating thing is still new with Charlie. I'm still thinking of Charlie as a friend. I need to think of him as a date. Maybe after a few dates that feeling will appear. For now, I decide to ignore the missing feeling.

CHAPTER 31

I PULL UP TO THE STUDIO lot gate and give the security guard my name. He looks on a list, smiles, draws a bright red line on a map for me to follow, and I'm on my way. I feel my heart start to tug as I drive by the big green building where Alexander filmed part of a movie. I remember how he had the craft service guy make a special cake, just like the one we had on our first date at the Italian restaurant.

I purposely look the other way and focus on finding the building highlighted on my map, where I'm supposed to meet Charlie as he finishes up a photo shoot with one of his biggest clients, Miranda Cossell. She has a reputation for being a bad girl (or so that's what's in the tabloids) and has been getting into trouble lately. Charlie's boss had him attend the photo shoot to make sure she didn't mess up anything.

I pull into an empty parking spot next to a sign that reads Reserved for Taylor Swift with a red BMW convertible in front of it. I roll my eyes. I do a quick check in my rearview mirror to make sure my makeup is okay and then walk up to the door. Looking to make sure the red light outside is off, I slowly pull it open. Once my eyes adjust to the much darker room inside, I see a short man with headphones who is glaring at me.

"This is a closed set, lady," he barks. "I suggest you get out of here, unless you want to be escorted out." I can barely hear him over the Katy Perry music.

I stand a little taller and try to hide my frown. "Yes, Charlie said it would be. Can you pl—"

"There's no Charlie here, lady. Seriously, I'm about to call security." He reaches down to push a button on the receiver that's attached to his belt, covers his mouth with his free hand, and says something into it. "Security is on the way," he barks at me.

I weigh my options—I can leave and call Charlie on his cell, though judging by how loud it is, I'm not sure he'll hear his phone. Or I can wait for security to get here and explain to them who I'm looking for. Before I decide what to do, Charlie slides out from behind a black curtain.

"Liv! I thought you might be the crazy lady security was coming for." Charlie wraps an arm around me. I glance at the short man and see his face redden. "Come on in, we've got one more wardrobe change and then I'm done." He guides me past the little man and through the curtains.

Once we are on the other side, I'm amazed at what I see. It's a gorgeous set of a tropical plantation, complete with lush green plants, real-looking grass, palm trees, a hammock, and a façade of an old wooden plantation with a wraparound porch. The windows to the façade even have bright red flowers in their flower boxes. It feels as though I have been magically exported to another country in another time. Charlie sees the awe in my eyes.

"It's pretty awesome, isn't it?" His boyish smile beams. "Two weeks after they finished filming, a horrible storm came through the town and completely wrecked the old home. The studio had to build this mock-up for the scenes that needed to be reshot. It's amazing how similar it looks to the original." He points to the photos of the original building that are pinned around the set, out of the camera's view. I nod in agreement. It really does look exactly the same. "So we're doing the publicity photo shoot here."

"This is amazing," I tell him. "Is the entire cast at the shoot?"

"They did cast shots yesterday. These are for Miranda. She tends to have, umm, special needs."

"Charlie! Charlie!" A female voice calls from the other side of the faux plantation. The voice is getting louder as we walk toward the front of the set. "I need you to call this guy. He's from some magazine you scheduled an interview with, and he keeps asking questions that I don't think I'm supposed to answer." Her voice trails off as we round the corner, and she sees me with Charlie.

Miranda Cossell is quite the sight. Her long blond hair is pulled up into a line of rollers, and there's a young woman who seems to be dabbing her chest and neck with wet cloths. Her robe is loosely tied around her waist, and she's sitting with her long, sculpted legs crossed and tilted to the side. A *Vogue* balances on her too-thin thighs. She wrinkles her brow and starts to move her right foot up and down rhythmically.

"I thought this was a closed set." She looks at me from head to toe and back up again. "I didn't realize you were bringing your little sister."

Little sister? Wow. This is clearly someone who doesn't like to share the spotlight.

"Miranda, this is my girlfriend, Olivia," Charlie explains. I am about to lean forward and put my hand out for her to shake when Charlie subtly puts his arm around me and pulls me to his side, saving me from her bite. "She's a big fan of your work, and we have a date tonight, so I thought I'd bring her by to meet you and watch a real pro at work."

Her foot stops moving, and she slouches a little. "Okay then. Make yourself at home." She says this last part as she opens her magazine and flips through it. She may as well have been talking to the models in the pictures.

Charlie leads me to a chair a few feet away from Miranda, sits down next to me, and gives me the that boyish grin.

Then it occurs to me, he called me his *girlfriend*. Does that mean he thinks I'm his girlfriend? *Am* I his girlfriend? This is only our third date, technically. Maybe he just said that to get Miranda to leave me alone. Do I even *want* to be his girlfriend? Maybe he just meant girl-*friend*. Should I say something? Or should I pretend it's nothing? Maybe I should act like I didn't even hear it. Yes, that's what I'll do.

"Sorry Liv, I've gotta take care of this real quick," Charlie whispers in my ear. "This jerk at *People* is asking Miranda the questions he was specifically told he couldn't. I've gotta fix it before she says something stupid." He kisses me on the forehead and stands next to Miranda. Not at all interested in Miranda's colorful past, I turn and continue to admire the set, comparing it to the pictures posted nearby.

I am in awe at how identical the plants are to the ones in the photographs. I'm wondering how the set designers get the palm trees to turn the same way, change colors in the same places, and flutter in the fake breeze just like in the photos, when my attention is drawn away. A tall guy in all black comes scuttling across the set, calling to Miranda.

"Hey girl!" he skips over to her and air-kisses her on both cheeks. "I'm here to do you up, but as usual, you look beautiful as is." He shakes his head at her as she folds her magazine and smiles at him like a puppy waiting for more praise. "You've really got to tell them to stop paying me to ugly you up, girl; you are just so gorgeous on your own."

Miranda smiles, and I half-expect her to start cooing. The man in black shoos the woman with the wet cloths away and turns Miranda's head from side to side, gently holding her face.

"I'm so glad you're here, Max. The last makeup guy made me look like a tramp. We have to reshoot the entire day."

"Well, that's because few people know true beauty when they see it. You need nothing but natural-looking color, dear. Only the best for the best." They both look at each other and smile.

I look to Charlie and he's on his cell phone and doesn't look happy. Max starts pulling all sorts of brushes and bottles and sponges out of a toolbox. He's looking around for something when his eyes fall on me.

"And who might you be, darling?" Though he uses the word "darling," I doubt that he means it.

"That's Charlie's *girlfriend*," Miranda chimes in.

Max looks at her. "Oh, well, I didn't realize. Next time I'll be sure to bring my boyfriend to work with me." He looks back at me and winks where Miranda can't see. He turns to Miranda. "Well maybe she can learn something from watching us." They both giggle like little girls.

I want to get up and go for a walk, but am afraid that if I leave my seat, the little man with the headset will pounce on me and throw me out so I stay.

"So…how was your date last night with the man?" Max asks Miranda.

"Sucked. He cancelled, the loser."

Max steps back and looks at her. "What? No one cancels on Miranda Cossell. He must be insane. I thought your first date was perfection." Charlie is still on the phone but I can tell he is half-listening to Miranda's story.

"So did I. Then the loser called and said he realized he's not over his last girlfriend, and it wouldn't be fair to lead me on." She rolls her eyes. "It's not like I want to have his babies. I'm just bummed I won't be showing up to the award shows on his arm."

"That would have been amazing." Max shakes his head. "Everyone would have been talking about that for months…Miranda Cossell and Alexander Young."

I feel the blood drain from my face, and my palms get all sticky. If I didn't know better, I'd swear my heart stops.

Charlie hangs up and looks at me. Miranda looks in the mirror to see Max's progress. Max looks at me and puts a hand on my knee. "What's the matter, darling? You look like you've seen a ghost."

A woman with a headset comes over to check on Miranda and let her know that the final shoot will begin in five minutes. Suddenly

Miranda is surrounded by people with clothes, brushes, water bottles, and all sorts of gadgets. Charlie is lost on the other side of the crowd, and I am thankful.

I take a minute to gather myself and digest what I've just heard. Why would he date Miranda Cossell? She's shallow and a party girl, and the woman wouldn't know what charity was if it hit her between the eyes. And is he really *not* over me? That's the whole reason he wouldn't go out with her again, right? So if he's not over me, then why isn't he with me?

CHAPTER

32

TODAY IS THE DAY. I am getting myself back on track, jumping head first into my work. And the best place to start, I've decided, is by going to my office. First I throw away all the magazines I don't need—*Redbook*, *Glamour*, *Self*, and any others that I was reading to avoid work. Next I throw out soda cans and junk food from my cupboards and fridge—also distractions to avoid work. Finally, I pull out my most recent folders with notes for potential clients. Well, at least they *were* potential clients when I used to return calls and was being proactive.

Hopefully a very friendly call and some enthusiastic stories of successful meetings will restore their faith in me. As I move the top folder, lying there in wait is THE note—The one Alexander found that ended our relationship. Well, I suppose the note didn't end our relationship, my business ended it. And if I'm being honest, it was really my lack of honesty about my business that ended our relationship.

Regardless, the note reminds me of some unfinished business, which I've been dreading. I need to call Clara and let her know why Alexander wasn't there that day at the car wash. More importantly, I need to let her know why I haven't returned her calls to set up another meeting.

I take a deep breath, close my eyes and wait for her to answer.

"Hello," Clara says. I can hear two kids screaming in the background.

"Clara, it's me, Olivia." I try to calm my voice. "Is now a good time to chat?" Inside I'm sort of hoping she says that it's not. But procrastinating will only make it worse. As I learned with Alexander, being upfront is the best way to go. Especially with people I care about.

I hear her mask the phone and say something to someone. The screaming becomes more distant.

"Sure, I can talk. I haven't heard from you in a while. Is everything all right?"

"Yes," I say, "but there is something that I want to talk to you about."

"Oh? Do you have plans for another meeting with Alexander Young?"

Hearing his name stings. Again, I take another deep breath. "It is about Alexander Young. But it's about the previous meeting, actually. There is something I need to tell you."

"Okay," she says. "Did I miss him because I didn't follow your directions properly?"

"No. You followed my directions just fine. Perfect, actually."

"Then what is it?"

"I gave you the wrong directions, Clara." I get it out quickly.

"Well," she pauses, "that's okay. We can try again."

"I mean, I gave you the wrong directions...on purpose."

"I'm not sure I'm understanding," she says, her voice still calm.

"See, Alexander is…*was* a personal friend of mine. And when you asked to meet him, I was caught off guard." I pause, waiting in case she has anything to say. All I hear is silence, so I continue. "Truthfully, I felt like I was betraying Alexander by arranging a meeting for you with him. Since I know…*knew* him so well. But I also felt like not arranging the meeting would be betraying you."

"So you sent me to a place you knew he wouldn't be?"

"Yes. Sort of."

"But the car wash was information that I gave to you. How did you know he wouldn't be there?"

Either I tell her the truth and hope for the best or I keep going with the half-truth. But I can't. It's Alexander. Lying about him now, even if it's not *to* him, would mean I haven't learned a thing from our breakup.

"I knew he wouldn't be there because he was with me," I blurt out.

"Wait, Alexander was out with *you*?" Her voice slows, as she begins to put the pieces together.

"Yes." I really want to change the subject. "I feel really bad about it. I can either give you your money back or I'll arrange your next meeting on the house. That is, *if* you want me to arrange another meeting for you."

"So you were actually out somewhere with Alexander Young?" Clearly, she does *not* want to change the subject.

"Yes." I don't think she actually heard the last part I said.

"As in, just you two?"

"Yes," I say again.

"Olivia?" Her voice is soft now, but I sense a hint of restraint. "Are you *dating* Alexander Young?"

"Yes. Well, I was. That—" How do I explain to my best client that while I'm supposed to be able to arrange spectacular meetings with celebrities for my clients, I can't even arrange to keep my celebrity boyfriend.

The only thing that makes me less credible than dating a celebrity, is being dumped by one.

"You have got to be kidding me! I can't believe you are dating him. I mean, I'm not surprised at all that you are dating him. You're beautiful, and smart, and know what celebrities want. It makes perfect sense." She doesn't sound angry at all. In fact, she sounds rather amused.

Before I have a chance to even think about how to respond, she starts talking again.

"I just can't believe that I know Alexander Young's girlfriend. I'm actually *friends* with Alexander Young's girlfriend. Can I tell everyone back home that I'm friends with Alexander Young's girlfriend? I promise I won't mention a word to any potential clients."

This is so much harder than I thought it would be. And for completely different reasons.

"Well, actually, about that." I swallow hard. "We aren't dating anymore. We seem to have some...differences in morals." I let her interpret that however she likes.

"Oh." Then silence.

After a few moments I ask, "Are you still there?"

"Yes," she says quietly. "I'm so sorry, Olivia. It must not be easy, with him all over magazines and...I'm just sorry."

"Thank you, Clara."

"So, who should we arrange a meeting with next?"

I'm on my way to the deli down the street from my office when Charlie calls.

"I was wondering if you want to grab lunch," he says into the phone coolly.

I really don't want to grab lunch with Charlie. I'm regretful that things went the way they did. He is such a great friend, and I don't want to lose that. But I also don't want to be involved with him, at least not the way he wants, at least not right now. Maybe if Alexander hadn't been in the picture I would have fallen for his understated confidence and insistence on being a gentleman, regardless of the situation. Chivalry is certainly appealing.

On the other hand, I can't avoid him for the rest of my life. I would miss our regular bar nights with Maria and Preston. Regardless of how this ends, I have to meet him for lunch.

"Sure. I'm headed to the deli down the street. The one that has the delicious—"

"The one that has the delicious meatball subs with the homemade marinara?" he interrupts.

"Yes, that's the one. Are you nearby?"

"Close enough. I'll see you in a few."

I order two meatball sub sandwiches and find an empty table outside, sipping my iced tea and waiting for Charlie to arrive. After ten minutes he pulls into a parking spot and joins me. I get up to hug him; he hugs me with only one arm. Maybe he is on the same page as I am after all.

"I have been wanting one of these for so long," he says as he takes a big bite. Marinara drips down his chin, and I start to giggle.

"What?" he asks, not waiting for me to answer before he takes another bite.

"You have—" I point to his chin and giggle again.

"I know! That's what makes it so good." He takes another bite. "Seriously, try it." The marinara is still on his chin. It's sliding farther and farther down, threatening to make the leap to his shirt.

I can't help but laugh.

"Okay," I say and take a big bite, not really caring where the marinara sauce goes. I can feel it drip down the side of my chin and plop onto the wrapper.

"See? Wasn't that delicious?" he asks.

It kind of was. I smile at him and take another bite, bigger this time, really letting the sauce go wherever it may. A big drop lands square on my light blue top. I look down at it, my lips puckered tight to keep any more sauce from escaping. Then I look back at Charlie. He has stopped eating and is just looking at me, his big goofy grin across his face. He hands me a napkin.

"It'll be okay. Just wipe it off and put one of your scarves on."

I shrug my shoulders and laugh.

We talk about work, and he asks how I'm feeling about getting back to arranging meetings. Then I ask about his work and if he's been to any fun events in the past week. We talk about nearly everything while avoiding the one thing we both know we need to talk about. Us. Once our food is gone, our drinks finished, and we've thoroughly wiped our faces, we have no choice but to say what we both know we came here to say.

"I'm sorry I haven't been calling you," he starts.

"It's okay. I know you've been busy." I try to deflect the conversation.

"Right, but really it's been more than just that."

"Oh?" I ask, wanting to hear what he has to say, though not really sure I do.

"Olivia, you know I care about you. I mean, I've known you since you were a baby. And I've watched you grow into this beautiful, smart young woman." He stops for a moment, as if he's not sure he wants to go on.

"Is this where you tell me I'm like a sister to you?" I smile at him, teasing.

"No," he says matter-of-factly, "you're definitely not like a sister to me. Honestly? I'm crazy about you. I would do anything for us to be together."

My smile is gone, and I'm not sure how to respond to this. Yes, we have been dating, but he has never been so forward about his feelings. I figured I was just a whim he was entertaining. But I should have known better. Charlie is a gentleman. He would never risk ruining our friendship over a fleeting feeling.

"But more than that," he continues, "I would do anything to make you happy. That's really all I want, to see your smiling face. Even if I'm not the one who's making you smile."

"What exactly are you saying, Charlie?"

"I'm saying that I guess I didn't really believe how in love you were...*are* with Alexander. All the signs might have been there, I just didn't want to see them. But after I saw your face when you heard Miranda mention him, I couldn't ignore it anymore."

I swallow hard. I didn't come here to talk about Alexander. I came here to talk about how I don't want to ruin our friendship. But he's right. I am still in love with Alexander, even if I can't be with him. That's what this is really about. Charlie and his bright blue eyes and gentle hands never stood a chance.

"As long as I've known you, I've never seen you as happy as you were with him. Now I know that. Even if you two aren't together right now, I know you should be with him."

Even if we aren't together *right now?* Well at least *he* hasn't lost hope.

"You're not saying anything," he prompts.

I'm not sure what to say. He obviously cares a lot about me. And here I am, throwing that away because I love someone else, someone who isn't currently speaking to me. So I say what I planned to say before he got here.

"We'll still be friends, right? Just like before? No weird whispering behind each other's backs?"

He laughs. "No more than before."

"You're the best, Charlie. You know that?"

He opens his mouth as if to say something but doesn't. Instead, he stands up and pulls me to my feet, wraps his arms around me, and gives me a real hug this time.

I sit down on my sofa with a huge pile of tabloids. I have a lot of catching up to do. After spending the day returning client calls, I've got a long list of celebrities I need to research. I've stocked up on coffee and snacks and am ready to spend my Friday night reading and taking notes. In fact, it's probably what my Friday nights will look like from now on. Be that as it may, I'm actually excited.

After meeting Brad Griffin on the hike, I've been filled with this irresistible buzz, the same buzz I felt when I first started my business. This buzz is the only thing that has helped me survive the whole Alexander misery thing. My mind is racing with all sorts of new ideas to try out.

Things will be different now though. They have to be. After living through what I put many of my celebrities through, I know I have to make some changes. If I've learned anything, it's that celebrities are humans. And they should be treated that way. So while planning meetings, I will take the celebrities' feelings into serious consideration. Meeting in the produce section at the grocery store—still okay. Bumping into a celebrity who's grabbing a coffee after his weekly therapy session—not so much.

Since a celebrity's need for normal interactions with normal people is what allows me to stay in business, I've decided to grant them some reprieve in this respect. If a date appears to be in progress (even without physical contact), the meeting will be postponed immediately. It's the least I can do to help the celebrity keep that part of his life normal.

And finally, although my bank account may take a hit, I will no longer offer follow-up meetings. I am not a matchmaker.

The time spent considering how my actions affect others has been hard. Figuring out how to continue my business while respecting other's privacy has been even harder. I wish I had done things differently with Alexander, but I didn't. And I can't change that now.

How I wish Alexander were by my side. But I, of all people, know that if you sit around waiting for a celebrity to remember you, you'll be alone for a very, very long time. So for now, I am jumping head first into this pile of tabloids and burying myself in my work.

I pop open a bag of almonds and start munching as I flip through a magazine. First I read an article about Channing Tatum and his secret obsession, which doesn't help me at all. Then I flip to the page with pictures from the most recent galas. There it is. The photo of Miranda Cossell and Alexander on their one date. I think about turning the page, but I don't. Instead, I give myself a minute to wallow. I focus on the photo. Her long legs peeping out of her gown. Her arm wrapped snuggly into the crook of his.

Then I notice something. Perhaps it's my imagination, or maybe my work mode is getting revved, but he's not looking at the camera. And he's not *really* smiling. *Her* smile extends from cheek to cheek, sure, but he looks rather bored. His arm, the one that's holding hers, looks tense, as if he doesn't want to touch her. The other arm is hanging limply at his side. His gaze isn't focused on anything. *She* is staring with all her might into the camera. Her beauty is so all-encompassing that most wouldn't notice he *isn't* smiling into the camera as well.

Okay. That's enough wallowing and dreaming. Back to work.

I find an interesting article on Liam Hemsworth and how he got into acting. Not particularly useful but interesting.

I'm interrupted by three quick knocks at my door.

It's probably Maria stopping by to try and convince me to join her, Preston, and Charlie at James Beach. I can't with all the work I have. I hop off the sofa and open the door.

It's not Maria.

"Hi," Alexander says in that sexy voice I miss so much.

I remind myself to breathe as I hold the door handle tight to steady myself.

"Hi," I respond. We both stare at each other for a moment. "Do you want to come in?"

He takes a few steps, and I turn to motion for him to sit. As I see the tabloids stacked on the table, panic enfolds me. Then I remember, he knows. I turn back to him and just shrug my shoulders.

"Sorry it's so messy. I wasn't expecting...anyone."

He puts his thumbs in his pockets. "Work?"

"Yeah," I say as I close the tabloid. "So what brings you by?" I really want to run across the room and jump into his arms, but I know I can't.

"It's good to see you," he starts and then hesitates. "I was hoping we could talk."

I nod, unable to speak without giving way to tears that are about to burst from my eyes.

"I ran into Charlie at an event the other day. At first I didn't want to hear what he had to say. But all this time...I've been looking for reasons and answers, and I just couldn't...I just couldn't understand why you did what you did. You seemed so *real* to me. So *normal*. It was too hard for me to believe that our whole relationship was a game to you."

"It wasn't," I interrupt.

He gently raises one hand a little, asking me to let him speak.

"Then Charlie told me everything. About how he saw you that first night we met, and he said you were giddy. And how everyone told you to use me to gather information but you wouldn't. How you struggled with not telling me about your business all along. Now I know that Clara is one of your most important clients and you need to keep her happy, and you lied to her to keep me out of your business."

I nod my head, barely believing what I'm hearing.

"He also said," his voice softens as he walks toward me, "that he's never seen you so in love as you were with me. He told me I was stupid for breaking up with you, and that I'm losing the best woman I'll ever meet."

I swallow, trying to keep my emotions in check, my tears from streaming down my cheeks.

"I think he's right. I was a fool to not hear you out. I'm sorry."

He steps closer, so he is only inches away from me. He takes his index finger and raises my chin so I'm looking directly into his eyes. "Can we try this again?"

I want to lean in and kiss him and forget anything ever went wrong. But instead, surprising myself, I take a step back. His eyes tense with worry.

"What about my work?" I ask. "How can I keep my business if you don't approve of it? It's my life, and I won't give it up."

"I know. I want to learn about it. I want to know *every part* of you. I hear you've worked magic for your clients over the years." He pulls a folded piece of paper out of his back pocket. "And I have this for you."

I unfold it carefully, as if it's a relic from the past. I can't believe what I'm looking at. At the top of the paper is Alexander's name. Below it are a bunch of basic, mostly well-known facts about him. Below that is a list of places that he tends to frequent, along with the days he's normally there.

"What's this?" I ask, confused.

"That's my life. My public life. You can use anything on that page to set up meetings with your clients. And don't tell me. I want their experience to be authentic. I want to think of them as the average girl. Just like when I met you."

While I'm having a hard time believing what is happening, it feels very real to me. This is the Alexander I fell in love with.

I feel my shoulders relax. "Really?"

"Yes, really. I want you in my life. I want us to get back to normal."

I throw myself into his open arms. He leans down, gently caresses my cheek, and kisses me like he hasn't seen me for years.

I guess Preston and Charlie were right, after all. I really am just the average girl.

EPILOGUE

CLARA AND I SIT IN the library parking lot, anxiously awaiting her meeting.

"Are you sure you're okay with this? I mean, he is your boyfriend," she says, her accent coming through when she says, "boyfriend."

"Absolutely," I reassure her. "He is totally fine with my business. And he will have no idea that you're a fan. I haven't said a word to him about it."

"Okay, if it's really fine." She lets out a big sigh. "I can't believe I'm going to meet Alexander Young. I can't believe he's your boyfriend." She opens her hands, palm up, in her lap, as if grasping an imaginary beach ball.

I glance at my watch. "It's time for you to go in. He should be coming in at about five. That should give you enough time to—"

"To go and find a chair in the science fiction section, his one guilty pleasure. I know."

I smile at her. She is definitely prepared. "Go for it," I encourage her.

I watch her walk away from the car and head for the two front doors of the library. All I can do now is wait, wait for Alexander to arrive, wait for them to meet, and finally wait for her to leave the building and tell me all about it. I glance down at the clock. Only one minute has passed. No wonder I accompany my clients. This is torture, sitting helpless.

Just as I think I might die of boredom or anxiety, I see Alexander's car pull into the parking lot and head toward my car. I slink further down in my seat to hide. I purposely parked near the exit so he wouldn't see me. No! Go the other way! I'm about to turn on the car and put it in reverse when a car right in front of him pulls out.

I hold my breath, and he turns his blinker on. Phew. Once the car zooms away, he pulls into the parking spot and opens his door. He takes a stack of books from the back seat, the same books that sat on his nightstand this morning. He closes the door and looks around the parking lot.

I duck, hoping he can't see my license plates and mine looks like just another silver car to him. After a minute or so, I pop up, and he's disappearing into the library. I turn on the radio and switch it to the jazz station.

Why am I so nervous? I arranged three meetings last week alone, and they all went perfectly well. I wasn't nervous for any of those. If anything, I should be more relaxed than ever today. My best, most experienced client is meeting with my happy and friendly boyfriend. I know them both so well that I can practically play out the meeting in my head while they live it for real. Yet here I am, sitting in my car, a nervous wreck.

I grab *To Kill a Mockingbird* from under my passenger seat and start reading. Although it was only meant as a prop so I'd fit in, and

I had no intention of reading it, I find myself fully engaged and forget that I'm sitting in a library parking lot.

I have no idea how much time has passed when I hear shuffling outside my car. I look up to find Alexander, about ten feet away, staring at me. When he gets my attention, he tilts his head to the side, shaking it just a little, and he smiles that sexy smile. Then he walks back to his car, gets in, and drives away.

Of all the meetings I have ever planned, I have never been caught until now. How did he know I'm out here? Did Clara let it slip? Did he somehow know who she is? Did the meeting go okay? I feel the car getting smaller and smaller as I wait for Clara to return with news of how it went.

I plant my gaze on the library doors, intent to will her out. Finally, the door opens, and she's waltzing to my car, almost literally. I can see her smile—ear to ear—from all the way over here. When she reaches my car, she opens the door and bounces in.

"Wow!" she exclaims.

"How did it go?" I'm dying to know.

"You are so lucky to have a guy like him. He is so nice. I barely had to say anything, and he struck up a conversation with me."

That's my Alexander. Never too important to talk to anyone. "Was he onto us, do you think? Did he know you were with me?" I ask.

"I don't think so. He didn't act like he knew me or expected me to talk to him."

"So tell me what happened. I want to hear every detail."

"I was sitting there, pretending to read a book, and he came over to my section. I got up and went to look for more books like the one I was reading. Just like you told me to, I—" Clara and I sit in the car for twenty minutes, going over every single detail, just like two high school girls talking about their first crushes. When I drop her off at her car, parked by my office, she is as thrilled as I've ever seen her.

After going over a few files for interviews with clients scheduled for tomorrow and making some phone calls to gather details on potential meetings, I head home.

Turns out I had nothing to worry about. Clara knew what she was doing and was very calm about it. Alexander didn't seem to have any idea he was the celebrity for one of my meetings. But then how did he know I was in the parking lot?

When I get to my front step, I'm surprised to find a bouquet of flowers. I pick them up to breathe in their scent. I can tell they were handpicked. I pull off the card that's attached and open it. As I read it, I can't help but giggle. It says:

"To the World's Best Meeting Consultant,

I had no idea I was in the middle of a "meeting" until I found you in the parking lot. Don't ever stop what you're doing. You're fabulous at it.

Love,

Alexander"

★

About the Author

★

Angelina Goode started writing star struck poems and short stories as a teen and went on to develop her writing skills while earning her BA degree in Journalism and Creative Writing. She now lives on the outskirts of Los Angeles with her husband and two children.

To learn more about Angelina Goode, visit her website at
www.angelinagoode.com